OPUS 2020

Anthology

Walter E. Ledwith

Opus 2020
Copyright © 2021 by Walter E. Ledwith
ISBN: 978-1-970153-99-6

La Maison Publishing, Inc.
Vero Beach, Florida
The Hibiscus City
lamaisonpublishing@gmail.com

Acknowledgements

Thank you to the Writer's Windowpane critique group
for all their help and support.

STORIES

ONE ACT PLAYS

STORIES

Buonarroti's Arm

The rising sun has set the hills surrounding the City of Florence aglow. The air is rich with the hope of spring. The earth is humming with fresh growth breaking through the soil. This is the kind of morning all Tuscans love and why they never want to leave. But along with the new growth, the vines of discontent have spread amongst the people. There has been turmoil in the city for days. The rumors are rampant, and tempers are short but not enough to deter two young men, the heroes of this story.

The boys live in a district beside the workshops of the Cathedral of Santa Maria Del Fiori in Florence, Italy. Their families have lived there for generations, being the masons, carpenters, and artisans of the building projects of that great city. The boys have grown, played as children, and now work in the shadows of the great Cathedral and its incredible dome. Stefano is twelve years of age with Botticelli-like features. A smart, alert, and industrious lad who has always found work with the building crews and purveyors of the area. The boy's reputation grew by word of mouth, and soon their diligence and hard work paid off. No longer would they carry bricks for the masons and lumber for the carpenters. They found work with the artist and sculptors of the major studios of Florence. They would sweep the marble chips off the floor, mix and stir the paints or bring victuals for those who remembered to eat. They carried correspondences and gossip from one studio to another while reporting on the progress of competing artists. Stefano boasted to all of his friends that he and Magro served the hands that created the art which adorned the city.

Magro, so-called because of his boney frame, is ten years old with curly red hair and bright blue eyes. He is an eager, energetic lad and is Stefano's partner and constant companion. The two-year difference in age with Stefano was small, but the level of maturity great, and Magro deferred to Stefano's understanding of the world and its ways. Both of their grandparents had worked alongside Brunelleschi while building his dome. It was something of which they were very proud. Their pedigree anchored them to the illustrious city and its history. Stefano's father spent most of his career working at the Cathedral. It provided a good living for the family, and they were never in need. His mother was of solid country stock with a strong religious background. She was born into a world where life had a purpose, and she was a willing supplicant. Magro's family was much the same. His father was a plasterer for the Carte Della Lana, the Wool-Cloth Guild. His mother was from Fiesole. The rumor in the district was that the groom carried his bride all the way down the hill from Fiesole to their new home. Sometimes his father drank too much, and they argue loudly. We find the boy's beginning their day. It is April 26,1527, a bright, sunny, Tuscan morning.

******

Stefano pulls aside the curtain of his small bedroom and finds his parents talking in the kitchen. His mother greets him,

"Buongiorno Stefano, come, sit and eat."

"Buongiorno Stefano," said the father.

"The bread is hot, and the stew from last night is on the stove. Zio Tonio brought us fruit from his orchard this morning. It's in a bowl by the door. The peaches look good, only a little green. Come sit, sit with your father. It's not often we have him home during the day."

Stefano takes a peach from the bowl and sits across from his father, eating, listening.

"Stefano, be careful out there today. This world is crazy. Those fools are making a demonstration again. They're going to storm the Palazzo Vecchio. A man would be crazy to go up on a scaffold with those fools running around below.

"I know, Papa."

"First, it was the Medici[1] and the Pazzi killing each other. Then the crazy priest[2] and look! Here we are, in 1527, and this is still going on. They've sacked Rome, the Pope is hiding in the Castel Sant Angelo, and they're coming for Florence next. I say Filippo Strozzi is behind this." Stefano's mom places a bowl of stew with thick chunks of bread in front of him.

"Il Babbo, not to worry. I heard a magistrate on the street say it will be all over soon. He says the Medici are going to leave." Stefano ate while talking, soaking up the gravy with his bread.

"Don't they realize people have to work," the father says, frustrated. "And the weather is so good . . . we're losing days. Damm politics! People have to make a living."

"Maybe you should stay home with your father today, Stefano. How many days you get like that?"

"I'll be fine, momma. We'll stay in the back of the Piazza, out of the way. Nothing can happen to us. Besides, the man said it would be over soon. We can make good money carrying messages and food, more than on a regular day."

"You stay away from the crowd," she said, waving her

---

[1] Medici, Pazzi and Strozzi: ruling families of Florence.
[2] Savonarola, renegade priest burned at the stake in 1498.

finger, "stay far away, so they don't trample you underfoot."

"Yes, momma, we will."

Magro knocks on the door and comes into the kitchen. He sees the fruit by the door and helps himself. He takes a chair at the table to catch up on what's being discussed.

"Magro, how is your father? What is he up to?" Papa asked.

"He has plasterwork at the monastery, so he left early."

"I'm glad your father has chosen a profession out of the weather Magro. He is a smart man. How are your Mother and Nonna doing?" asks Momma.

Continuing what is an ongoing argument for them, Papa interrupts.

"I'm a mason Momma. I will always be a mason. Get over it."

The subject agitated momma as well,

"It would not be so big a change, and at your age — "

"Magro, we should go. It's getting late," Stefano said, pushing his chair underneath the table. Magro did the same. He took a courier's bag from a hook by the door, slipped it over his head and onto his shoulder. He gave Magro his bag and took a piece of fruit. Magro did the same.

"A piu tardi Momma, Addio Papa." Stefano said, leaving.

"Come home if you get hungry," Momma called after them, "and stay away from the crowd."

******

The boys enter the narrow, winding streets. The Romans built the old stone roads in the early days of the city. As they walk down the center, the smell of bread baking and the sounds of family life can be heard from both sides of the meandering, cavernous streets. The religious Icons on the cornices of the buildings were a constant reminder that heaven was watching. They pass the works department of Santa Maria Del Fiori, where scaffolding is neatly stacked, and numbered stones lie on the ground in rows, waiting to be placed. The green marble of the cathedral, set into the brick, glistens in the morning sun. They continue to San Lorenzo and the Medici library. The streets have become crowded. Like veins carrying blood to the heart, the old streets carry people from all directions to the Piazza Della Signoria, the heart of Florence.

"Magro, here with me," urges Stefano, hugging the building to stay clear of the river of people flowing by.

"I can hear the crowd yelling up ahead, Stefano. I've never seen so many people in my life. Maybe we should go back home."

"Just stay close. Here, give me your hand. We'll be fine. If we get separated, we will meet up at San Lorenzo's."

"Ooch! . . . Merda," cried Magro, "that man stepped on my foot . . . He's crushed it . . . wait!" He ducked into an alcove and took off his shoe to assess the damage. "He was big as a horse." Seeing that his foot was not broken, he put his shoe back on. "I guess it's okay."

"The Piazza is just ahead. We're almost there, so stay behind me, close to the buildings. We'll go to the back of the piazza where there are fewer people. I know a roof-top where we will be able to see everything. Stay with me, Magro."

They creep along past the closed shops on the way to the piazza. When they arrived, they saw the Palazzo Vecchio surrounded by people; some of them fighting. They creep along the perimeter of the crowd and work their way to the rear of the piazza.

When they reached the back of the crowd, Fra Angelico caught sight of them and waved them over.

"You boys should go home . . . there is no good to come of this."

"We were hoping to make a little money today Father," Magro says, speaking up.

"The Devil has entered these people, my son, and all they know is destruction. There will be no money made here today. You would do better to go home during this craziness. A mob is like an enraged bull, throwing itself about wildly. Only God knows which way it will turn next."

"Yes, Father, we will do as you say. . . . Magro, we can go this way. Thank you, Fra. Angelico."

"Give my best to your parents, boys, and I'll see you all in church."

The boys make the sign of the cross and continue on their way.

"Stefano, what are you doing? Home is in the other direction. You have lied to the priest."

"No, I haven't . . . we're just going to make a stop before we go home . . . I want to see what's going on. Andiamo Magro, it's this way to Russo's roof."

From the roof, the boys could see the entire piazza. Soldiers were fighting off a group of protesters in front of the Palazzo Vecchio. The rioters had taken control of the Signoria, and the occupiers threw anything they get their hands on out of the windows, down upon the soldiers below who were struggling to enter the building.

"Stefano," Magro said, pointing, "there is a big circle in the center of the crowd, with no people. Why are they doing that . . . why are they staying away?"

"That's where they burned the crazy priest. It's bad luck."

"Oh, Dio" Magro says with a gasp, making the sign of the cross over his heart. The chaos before him was an eerie scene which he wished would go away, but with no luck. Vultures hovered above the piazza, never a good sign. The people below are so loud he can barely make out the bells of the Cathedral tower. The sun is high in the sky, but it does not penetrate the clouds of hate below.

"Maybe we should go Stefano . . . This roof is boiling hot, and I'm scared."

"Just a while longer . . . then we can go," Stefano says, not taking his eyes off the turmoil. "I'm getting hungry anyway, so just a little longer."

"Stefano, look!" Magro screams, "Look, look!"

"Look at what? What! What do you see?"

"A man threw a bench from the window, and it hit the statue of David . . . it broke his arm . . . David has only one arm. Stefano, why did they do that?"

"Holy Mary Mother of God . . . Look at that . . . merda[3] What have they done? They're fighting all around the David. They don't even see what's happened. We have to think Magro. What are we going to do?" Stefano paces the parapet wall, thinking, watching. "Oh, . . . good, they're moving to the other side of the big doors, away from the David. But now the statue of Hercules is in trouble!" A look of recognition sweeps across his face. Stefano has come up with a plan.

"Magro, we have to pick up the pieces. Remember when Marcello knocked over his statue, and we had to pick up the pieces so he could put it back together again? We have to do that; we have to collect all the pieces so it can be put back together."

---

[3] Shit

"But it's so crowded down there, and your mother said not to get trampled on."

"We'll wait till it calms down. They have to eat and drink like everyone else. We should wait a little longer . . . They look like they might be getting tired."

The boys settle in on Russo's rooftop for several hours. Watching, biding their time, waiting for their chance to carry out their plan. Stefano sees that he has to keep his partner's spirits up. Magro has a brave heart, but the madness has overwhelmed him. He has curled into a ball behind the parapet wall, covered in a shroud of foreboding.

"Magro, we will stay to the outside of the crowd. The same way we came until we are close to the statue of David. We can stop and rest awhile to get ready for what we have to do. We will put the pieces we collect into our bags. Hopefully, they haven't been kicked around too much. Be sure to get them all. If we get separated, we'll meet at San Lorenzo's chapel. If I'm not there already, wait for me."

"Let's get on with it then. I'm hungry."

******

The boys work their way along the edges of the crowd. The closer they get to the Signoria, the more agitated the people around them become. They duck into doorways and watch for opportunities to move forward.

"Magro, come," Stefano says, jumping two doors down. "This is Mauro's house. This is where I bring his letters."

They open the iron gate and enter Mauro's courtyard. There is a full-sized statue of the Good Shepard in the center, looking as though he were hiding from his flock. The boys climb the gate to it's top to see what's going on in the piazza.

"Stefano, there are more people now than before. From every direction, they are still coming."

Looking over the heads of the crowd, Stefano could see the David clearly. Though wounded, the Shepard was angry and defiant as he looked towards Rome. The boys are speechless, wide-eyed, and fearful as they watch all that is happening before them. They had never seen people act like this before. Stefano recognizes familiar faces in the crowd. Nice people who he had worked for and come to know. Now they are crazed and full of rage. He will never see them the same way again; his innocence and naivete had been shattered and broken. They lie scattered on the ground, just like David's arm. He feels he has lost something.

The Priest was right. The mob is a wild and frantic bull, angry and driven by hate.

"Maybe we should go now, before more people come" Stefano says climbing down. They both agree the time to act has come. Opening the gate, Stefano gives his last instructions.

"Grab the back of my belt and stay close. Hold on if you can. Remember . . . San Lorenzo afterwards. . . . Look for the tower to find your way," he shouts as they disappear into the crowd.

It is not long before Magro has to relinquish his grip on Stefano. The push and pull of the demonstrators are too much for him, and he is swept away on the crest of a wave.

"Magro, keep talking so I know where you are. . . . We're almost there."

The boys weave in and out of the surrounding giants like fish in a school, maintaining their distance, never colliding.

"Here it is," Stefano yells when he reaches the statue. "We made it. . . . You pick up the small pieces . . . I'll gather up the arm." He takes the hand holding David's deadly sling and puts it into his bag. He finds the forearm, veins bulging, and a smaller section of the upper arm which he hands to Magro.

"Here, take this . . . It's time to go. You first . . . and be careful!"

"Which way should I go? I only see people!"

"Look up. . . . see the tower? Go that way. Andiamo Magro, we must go . . . now!"

Stefano senses that the anger of the mob is growing and that they must get out of there right away. They weave their way in and out of the crowd like the salmon swimming upstream.

******

They arrive at San Lorenzo's together, and both collapse under its archway with sighs of relief.

"We did it. We saved David!" laughs Stefano, amazed at their accomplishment. They sit, examining the parts of David's arm before them. The unbridled chaos outside the chapel's courtyard fades as they both study Michelangelo's work. Stefano examines the forearm, turning it, tracing every vein with his fingers.

"Look at the veins and the muscles on this arm. . . . It almost looks alive, so real I expect it to bleed."

Magro, measuring his hand against that of the giant, is amazed.

"It's so big, and he has very long fingers," he mumbles, musing over the hand of Israel's greatest champion.

The youths gather the parts together and head off to Stefano's house. When they reach Santa Maria del Fiori, there are fewer people on the streets, and everything seems as it normally would. The setting sun reflects on the orange tiles of the cathedral, and the bells of Giotto's tower ring crisp and clear. Children are running about playing hide and seek behind the building materials in the storage yard. A small dog ferrets them out, giving away their hiding places, despite their protestations. The narrow streets sing with the clanking of pots and pans. The sweet aromas of the evening meals being prepared weigh heavily in the air as the boys get closer to home. They reach Stefano's house and open the thick wooden door. They enter the kitchen and find Mamma and Papa just as they left them in the morning.

"Magro, your mother was here looking for you. She says you should go home for dinner."

"Thank you, Signora Lanza. I will go right away . . . I'm starved," he says, placing his section of the arm on the table. He hangs his satchel on the back of the chair and leaves. Stefano rests the forearm on the table and removes the sling hand from his bag, setting it beside the other parts. The three of them stand silently, trying to comprehend what's before them.

"What is this?" Papa says, clutching his head in his hands, "this looks like the work of 'Il Divino," he cries with fear in his eyes. "What has happened?"

Stefano tells his parents about the events of the day and all that they had seen.

"Everyone was acting crazy! They stopped being people and became a pack of wild dogs."

Papa sits, hypnotized, examining the parts of Michelangelo's statue. Momma is visibly upset listening to Stefano tell his story.

"They could have killed you!" Momma exclaims, white in the face. "You don't know these people. They killed Giuliano

Medici while he was taking communion, right at the altar, in the church, his family helped to build!"

"Were it not for Polizano the poet, they would have killed 'Magnifico'[4] as well," Papa says at the top of his voice. "Now this! . . . it is a sacrilege!"

"Stefano, I want you to stay near home. These men know only hate for the Medici. Even Michelangelo fears them." Momma speaks absolutely, leaving no room for discussion. "You are to stay near home till these men hang from the windows of the Signoria, like the Pazzi and that Bishop from Pisa." She returns to her cooking, leaving Stefano with his father.

"Son, I am very proud of you. All of Florence will praise you and Magro for your courage today. We will talk later about what we will do when your mother calms down. For now, we will find a safe place for these treasures."

Papa leaves Stefano at the kitchen table to further study the fragments of the great work of art. *Right here, on my kitchen table, I can't believe it,* as he revels in the details of the hand. Papa returns from his bedroom carrying a wooden box.

"This should be big enough for everything," he says and sets it on the table. "After dinner, we can place it under the floorboards beneath the table. The arm should be safe there until we figure out what to do."

Momma announces dinner is ready,

"Clear the table so we can eat."

Father and son pack the box carefully. Each take a handle and reverently place it in the bedroom. Silently, they wipe the table and set it for dinner. Momma serves chicken with sauce and pasta.

---

[4] Lorenzo de Medici

"We have spring radish and scallion, with vinegar and oil. Come on you two . . . wake up, mangiate!" Momma tries to make conversation, telling them the gossip of the day but fails to hold their attention. They eat everything on their plate, heartily, though silently. They finish dinner and clear the table. Momma cleans the dishes while Papa and Stefano move the table and lift the floorboards, exposing a cache of their most prized belongings. Papa opens up a small jewelry box and removes a heart-shaped locket. He puts it in his pocket, winking at Stefano. They make room for the wooden box and place Buonarotti's arm in the cache pit. Replacing the floorboards, they set the table over it and sit down with tea and biscotti to discuss their plans.

"We can't have this thing under the table for ever. What are you gonna do?" Momma asks.

"First, we are going' to wait for things to calm down. We should say nothing. Magro's family should say nothing as well. I will talk with Guido before he goes to work tomorrow morning and explain. There will be no trouble if we keep it to ourselves. Stefano, did you talk to anyone? . . . Did anyone see you with the David's arm?"

"I don't think so . . . They were too busy fighting."

"Good, good . . . I mean good that—"

"We know what you mean, Sandro, please, just go on," Momma says.

They continue their discussion until they all agree on a plan. The first week they will lie low. Go about their business as they normally would until the city returns to sanity. Then, maybe the second week, they would consult with the leaders of the Wool Guild to see how to move forward. The Wool Guild is in charge of the works dept of Santa Maria del Fiori, and they could make the necessary repairs to the statue.

Satisfied, they agree not to speak of the arm until it is time to act.

******

The turmoil continues for several days, and it is not until they elect a new gonfalonier and choose a Signoria[5] that the people believe the Medici have left. As the city returns to normal, people are talking of the damage caused by the uprising. All but a hardened few are troubled and distraught by the damage done to the statue of David, the symbol of Florentine independence. Only the most bitter amongst them welcome it as a slight to the Medici and their dominance. There is a cloud of shame hanging over the city, and throughout Florence, the people asked, "Where is the broken arm of the David."

Stefano and Magro remain in their district, busying themselves doing chores for friends and neighbors. They play with the children at the cathedral, inventing new games, becoming the leaders of great armies. They are happy, restoring some of the innocence lost the week before. After Mass on Sunday, the family takes a walk, greeting friends and neighbors, exchanging news and gossip. It is a beautiful day enjoyed by all. Walking home, Papa tells them he has made a decision.

"Tomorrow, we will go to the Wool Guild and make arraignments to return our cache to the city. We will have done our part, and I can return to work. Let Magro know, and I will tell Guido later. It is best that we do this together."

The next morning Stefano and his father talk as they walk to the Carte Della Lana.

---

[5] Governing body of Florence

"We will speak to Signor Lippi. He will know the best way to repair the David."

"But Il Babbo, Signor Peche is the head of the guild. Shouldn't we speak to him first?"

"When you tell Peche something, you might as well tell the entire world."

The offices of Carte Della Lana stand across from the Baptistry. As they approach, the sun casts a golden beam upon Ghiberti's bronze doors, illuminating paradise. Magro and his father are waiting for them in front of the Guild building. They agree that they should go in together for greater effect. Signor Cavalieri, the notary, is in the lobby, and Magro asks where he could find Signor Lippi.

"Ah, si, secondo piano, a destra."

"Grazie Signor," said Stefano.

"Prego ragazzi,"

They climb the wooden staircase to the second floor. Their footsteps echo in the rotunda above. Signor Peche greets them at the top of the stairs and tells them Lippi is in his office.

"I just left him. He's still there."

They find signor Lippi in his office. He is replacing an armful of books to his library shelves. The group encircles him, and in hushed tones, Papa tells him all that has happened.

"This is excellent news!" Lippi says with a sigh of relief. "You have done right in coming to me, Sandro. And boys, you have been very brave. Soon all of Florence will honor you!" He puts the books down, wipes his forehead with a handkerchief, and continues.

"This works out perfect! . . . If there can be such a thing after a tragedy like this, but Buonarotti has agreed to return to

Florence to help prepare the defenses of the city. I will send a message to inform him of this wonderful news! It is said he is very distressed over the damage to the statue of David. He will be very happy to hear of this." Signor Lippi shakes everyone's hand, thanking the boys once again for their service to the city. "Tell me," he asked, "Where is the arm now?"

"We have buried it outside the city walls," Sandro says, winking at his son. "We will bring it to the Signoria when the time is right."

"No, it would be best to bring it here. Arrivederci amici! We will speak again soon."

Talking amongst themselves in front of the building, the quartette agrees to continue their silence on the matter.

"I have to go to work now, and Magro, you have to help your mother . . . We will talk later, Sandro. Andiamo."

"Stefano, walk with me. I have to go to the Ponte Vecchio to pick something up."

"What have we to do with the gold merchants, Papa?"

His father takes the heart-shaped locket from his pocket and shows it to Stefano.

"My mother gave this locket to your Momma when we married. Her mother gave it to her, and Momma will give it to your bride when you marry. The chain broke some years ago, and now is the time to replace it. A little appreciation for all your mother does for us. And also, I want to see the David."

Papa is silent as he walks through the piazza. Charred furniture smolders in piles, debris is scattered about, and the piazza is deserted but for them. This part of the city has not yet recovered from the turmoil that has taken place. Papa approaches the David with a fixed stare. He walks around the giant, assessing the damage.

"This is not so bad, Stefano. The breaks are clean and should easily come together, . . . maybe with copper nails." He sees a chunk of marble lying at the base of the statue, picks it up, and hands it to his son. "This might be necessary later."

They continue on to the Ponte Vecchio to pick up the gold chain for Momma. The covered bridge smelled dank and moldy. Wine bottles and rotten food are strewn about everywhere. Drunk men lie in the corners and doorways, sleeping off their debauchery. Very few people pass through the old bridge and those that do cover their nose as they cross to the opposite side of the Arno. They reach the jeweler just as he is closing his shop. It is early, but he cannot stay open any longer. "Who would want to buy anything from this place" he says, pointing to the trash along the thoroughfare. The jeweler brings Momma's chain in a blue, fabric-covered box. Papa examines it, smiling his approval, pays him, and pockets Momma's regalo.

"Momma will love your gift, Papa, and the box is pretty too."

"It is from the both of us." Papa says, rubbing the top of Stefano's head. Papa, placing his hands on his hips, looks around and agrees with the jeweler,

"This place is disgusting . . . let's go home, Stefano."

They return the way they came, keeping to the center of the cobblestone road on the Old Bridge.

"Papa, why are these men sleeping here? If they are drunk, they should go home to sleep."

"I agree, Stefano, but they have no home here in Florence. Some come from far away for the opportunity they see in the turmoil of a troubled city. Some believe it a party, an excuse to drink and carry on. I am surprised the new Gonfaloniere has not chased them away. Perhaps he is afraid of them like they are in Rome."

"Il Babbo, the more I know, the less I understand."

"Me too, Stefano, me too. We're in paradise . . . and we're shitting all over the garden."

******

The city resumes its natural cadence as everyone returns to their regular schedule. It makes little difference to the laborer or the baker, which leading family reigns over them. The Signoria, now in charge, had not always performed well and is itself a role of the dice. What matters to the people of Florence is order and stability, so the wheels of commerce can turn and provide everyone with a livelihood.

Papa returns to the scaffolds, but not without difficulty. The weeks he spent at home has caused his joints to become stiff, and he doesn't move as freely as he would like to. The climbing of the scaffold, walking on the planks, and placing the stones, takes its toll by the end of the day. He is sore and sometimes in pain. He is keeping his problem from the family, not wanting to worry them, and not yet ready to admit that Momma is right. Her voice repeats in his head,

"It's a young man's business. You're crippling yourself."

He knows she is right but must continue for now. He should wait a little longer to see if his condition is permanent. *It might be temporary*. The one thing he is sure of is that a loss of income is unacceptable. *I have made it through the week. Let's wait and see.*

Momma can sense Papa's discomfort and chooses not to aggravate him any further. She knows the pain will make this decision for him. Stefano has done well during the week with a brisk business in delivering packages and letters.

"Il Babbo, I've never had so many florins before. I hope business stays this good forever."

"Feast or famine mio filo! Learn to save, and you'll be as rich as the Medici." They all laugh at the likelihood of that happening. There is a knock on the door, and Stefano jumps to answer it.

"Signor Lippi, Bonasera!"

"Good evening Stefano, is your father at home?"

"Yes . . . Please come in."

"Signora Lanza," he says, taking off his hat and crossing the room. "Sandro, we have to talk."

"Of course, of course, please sit down. Stefano, bring the good table wine and a glass for Signor Lippi."

"No . . . no thank you, Sandro."

"Perhaps the gentleman would like tea and biscotti?" Momma asks, "The kettle is warm?".

"That would be delightful, Signora Lanza." Sitting across from Papa, he continues.   "Sandro, the maestro has notified me he will arrive in Florence on Sunday. He asks your permission to come by here to thank you and the boys personally for your service."

"Here! . . . Il Divino!"

"Yes, and he will bring a cart with a porter to collect the arm of his David."

"Momma! Do you hear that! Michelangelo will come here, . . . to our house!"

"Dio mio, I can't believe this. In our own home, . . . here, Michelangelo. God is smiling on us today!" Momma says, raising her hands to the sky.

"Very well, . . . I will send word to the maestro," Lippi

says, biscotti in hand. " Ah Sandro, one other thing. Giuseppe Nero is retiring. He will be moving to the countryside . . . to the wife's family farm. We will need someone to take his place, keeping inventory and supplying our masons with what they need. I can think of no better man for the job than you. Would you be interested?"

Momma wipes her hands with a towel and joins them at the table, very interested in what Signor Lippi is saying. "After all, Sandro, working the scaffold is a young man's business."

Momma smiles at Papa, and he nods in agreement.

"When do I start?" Papa says, beginning to like the idea of a new job.

"On Monday. Giuseppe will show you everything you need to know, and we will take it from there."

The talk at the table is animated, and the room is alive with laughter and happy faces. On his way to the door, Signor Lippi reminds Stefano, "Don't forget to tell Magro to bring his parents on Sunday. The maestro wishes to meet them as well... Buona notte tutti!" closing the door behind him.

"This is wonderful!" Momma says, hugging her husband, then her son, laughing, almost crying. "My son will be honored by Michelangelo . . . and my husband will work with dignity. God is smiling on us today."

"Rosina, sit. Stefano and I have something to show you." Papa places the blue box on the table; Momma's eyes are wide with surprise. "We went to Carlo the jeweler and had a chain made for your locket." She takes the locket and chain from the box. Tears form in the corners of her eyes as she studies it.

"I've not seen this in so long."

Papa takes the chain and places it around her neck and

kisses the top of her head.

"Te amo mia sposa."

"Te amo Momma."

******

They spend Saturday preparing the house, and themselves, for their esteemed guest. The aroma of Momma's cookies and pastries sweetened the air. They wash the windows, the floors are cleaned, and everything is put in its place. Though humble, there is a stately quality to their home, and it is welcoming. A new bar of scented soap is brought out, and all three bathe on the same day. They set their best clothes outside on the line for a freshening in the breeze. Polite greetings and gestures, practiced amongst themselves, promise to go smoothly. Rumors throughout the quarter have been circulating all morning. A person of great importance will visit the neighborhood, but who and when was not known. When asked, Momma, Papa, and Stefano's answer is what they had agreed upon. "I know nothing about it."

******

It is a beautiful, sunny Sunday morning. After Mass, the two families walk together to Stefano's house to await their guest. Both families are wearing their best attire. This is noticed by the other churchgoers who attribute it to the mysterious visitor that everyone is expecting. Sandro and Guido walk in front, with their sons at their sides. The women follow behind with Magro's little sister, Eva. The curious parishioners keep a respectful distance, eager to know what's going on. Little Eve is keeping an eye on them as well,

"Momma, why are those people following us?" she asks.

"It is because you look like a princess in your new dress, Eve."

"Yes, they are correct . . . I am a princess."

Signor Lippi has joined them. The living room of Casa Lanza is full. The families talk, eat pastries, and boast of their courageous offspring. There is the sound of clopping hooves on the cobblestone pavement outside. Few horses travel these streets, and they know exactly who it is. There is grumbling and mumbling on the other side of the wooden door, and then a knock. Stefano opens the door to a gentleman a little taller than himself, with sad eyes and a rugged, worn face. His V-shaped beard is a little wild and showing gray. His attire is simple, without ornament or unnecessary frills. They are well-made clothes, tailored tastefully, and of excellent material. Behind the gentleman stands his servant, calming a donkey that is attached to a cart. People standing on the other side of the street congregate and debate what is going on. Handing the reins of his horse to his servant, the gentleman Introduces himself.

"Buongiorno, I am Michelangelo Buonarroti. Is your father at home?"

The boys, with a sweeping gesture, welcome him. He removes his hat and greets the people gathered. The room is crowded, and the illustrious Michelangelo fills the remaining space. Papa and Signor Lippi rush to bid him welcome.

"Maestro, you bring great honor to my home, come, please, make yourself comfortable."

"All of Florence welcomes you back home, maestro."

Lippi says, pulling out a chair from the table. Il Devino sits, hat in hand, salt and pepper hair disheveled, looking uncomfortable with all the attention he is receiving.

"Pastries maestro?" Momma asks, holding a platter of sweet treats.

"Hum," he says, studying them closely . . . "they look so good. But I can't signora, . . . it is too early for me to eat, so, . . . no. But if I could take some home with me, I would be very grateful. Often, I work late into the night, and I have to wake my servant to go find pastries to satisfy my cravings. With your generosity, he gets a good night's sleep, and I will have your delights to enjoy while I work." Seeing the expression on their faces, he laughs, "Not to worry. Enzo is well paid for it . . . and he makes out like a bandit."

The room erupts into laughter, and they have broken the ice. They talk freely, like old friends at a wedding. Stefano and Magro tell an animated tale, elaborating the dramatic story of the saving of the arm. There are *Ooh's* and *AHHAA's, grunts* and *groans*, from a captive audience, engrossed in the details told by the young thespians. There is much praise and many questions. Unusual for the maestro, he is the most talkative of all.

"And I wanted to meet the parents of such brave and steadfast young men. Ragazzi, though young, when everyone else was acting crazy, you kept your wits about you and did what needed to be done. Genitori, these characteristics don't happen by themselves. They have to be nurtured in the home, in the church, at the dinner table daily. Your skill at carving character and strength in a boy is equal to, or maybe greater than my hands holding a chisel. And your work walks and breathes! Tutti Bravi!" The maestro is as animated as the boys and talks excitedly. "Signor Lippi has told me how industrious you both are, and with your fathers' permission, I would like you to work for me. I have agreed to work for the Signoria on the defenses of the city and could use two smart assistants on the project."

There is a collective *Gasp* in the room, and the families thank the maestro profusely. Stefano and Magro leave and return with the old box and place it on the table. Michelangelo stands and removes the lid of the cache. He examines each piece, studying them closely.

"This is not bad . . .the clean breaks will make for good repairs . . . and it's all here. You have done well." Replacing the parts to the box, he continues, "I thank you, but I have to go. There is much to do before day's end." Grinning at the irony, he tells them, "I feel more comfortable here than at the Papal estates. I am reminded of my younger days in Arezzo. The closeness of family and friends, sharing the good times and the bad, . . . we were stronger together. None of the backstabbing politics you find in Rome." He walks to the door and calls out to his servant. "Enzo, take the wood box to the wagon and wait for me." Returning to the table, he is stopped by Momma placing pastries wrapped in a towel into the box.

"Make something beautiful, maestro." She blushed like a schoolgirl and stepped back with Papa. The maestro placed the lid on the box, set his hat, bid everyone good luck, and followed Enzo outside. He stroked his horse's main saying,

"I think I'll walk him home, Enzo. He has carried me enough for one day."

Michelangelo takes the reins and strolls down the cobblestone street, followed by Enzo and the donkey cart. The people who had gathered walked behind them, hoping to catch a glimpse of 'Il Divino.'

Epilogue

Stefano and Magro became Michelangelo's personal assistants. A scaffold had been built around the David, and the people of Florence watched with great interest, the restoration of the statue. The joining of the parts, the sanding, and polishing took several weeks as the maestro only accepted perfection. When the work was finished, and the symbol of the Florentine Republic restored, there were celebrations throughout the city. The Ponte Vecchio was strewn with banners. Food vendors set up in all the major piazzas. Musicians meandered through the streets playing music that celebrated the republic.

The boys continued with the maestro, surveying, repairing, and adding to the defenses of the city. Many times, they work late into the night and return home exhausted after struggling to keep up with Michelangelo's endless energy. Though difficult, they completed all of their tasks to the maestro's approval, and from that time on, they will assist him whenever he is working in Florence. They worked together for more than a year on the fortifications of their beloved city. Eventually, the city fell, and the Medici were restored. Fearing for his life, Michelangelo had to flee, leaving the work to be finished by his apprentices.

After this time, the reputation of the boys grew immensely, and they were sought after for all the construction projects of the city. Their reputation grew as they became men, and in the years to come, Stefano and Magro would become the premier construction consultants in Florence.

The mature Stefano became well established in the Carte Della Lana and an esteemed guild member. He bought a respectable house in the center of the city and took a wife. His bride, the daughter of a magistrate, was also active, working with various women's guilds and charities. It was a good marriage, and together they become leaders in the community. They had one daughter, lovely, gracious, and mannered.

Magro took the fruits of his labor and bought a working farm in Fiesole. He married a local girl, and together, they had eight bright and healthy children. The farm was well managed by a local family and produced a surplus every year. Every morning the family gathered at the door of their villa to see Magro off for the day. As the years pass, and the family grew, the cacophony of "Goodbye Papa" drowned out the bells of Giotto's tower below. Each morning Magro would mount his horse and ride down into the city, aware and grateful for his blessings and good fortune. Into old age, neither Stefano nor Magro ever tire of telling the tale of "Saving David."

An Anthropomorphic Observation
From the Trunk of my Jeep

There is a pair of Osprey working the lake this evening. They seem to enjoy themselves as they ride the amber solar winds. Hovering over the lake, they dive and skim the water like a stone gliding across a mirror. They look past their own reflection into the mysterious waters, searching for a glimmer of silver. The fish come to the surface looking for their own tasty morsel. The long-legged spiders walk upon the water, munching on dinner as they travel. The spider runs away, the fish returns to the abyss, and the Ospreys revisit their perch to wait for another opportunity. One of them drops down and circles the lake at a high speed, stirring the pot, so to speak. Sometimes flapping, sometimes gliding, scanning the water's surface for something shiny that can be taken home. I can see his excitement. This is what he is made for. Perfectly designed to see at great heights, he can calculate the distance and speed of his prey. He can coordinate his own movements to achieve his goal; to pluck from the grid we call space, his precious sustenance. This is his tai chi, and he is firing on all eight cylinders.

"You'll not get away next time silver food."

A bass has come close to the surface. He doesn't see any shadows on the glass ceiling, so he swims along happily, feasting on a cornucopia of tasty insects. There is no wind today. The water is calm; not a ripple except for the bugs on the surface. Perfect!

The osprey whistles then dives feet first towards the earth. Thirty… thirty-five… forty… forty-five miles an hour, he plunges fearlessly. The bass sees his shadow, but it is too late. Wide-eyed and helpless, he is yanked from the water.

"I can't breathe … there is nothing here to breathe." He silently screams, squirming, losing consciousness with each moment. Suddenly, he is falling. An eagle has tried to steal the osprey's prey. Feet first, back against the wind, almost upside-down, the eagle stretches out his long talons to reach the bass but fails to catch him. The bass slaps the water with a belly-flop, shocking him once again, but the water filling his gills brings life.

"I can breathe, I can breathe!" slowly coming back, gaining momentum, mustering the strength to dive deep below the surface where he will be safe. Then, a pair of talons snatches him from the water.

"No!... not again! I can't breathe. Where are you taking me? It's cold here. Oh shit! There are more of them. Don't put me in there. Stop... there eating me. You're not supposed to eat me. Where are the big one's? At least they don't eat meeeeee......"

The fledgling osprey chirp wildly in the nest as they feast upon their silver treat. Mom and Dad fly off into the orange glow. Returning to work one more time before nightfall.

The Shire

When my friends call from New York, and I tell them I am living in a trailer park in Florida, they imagine me in a rundown single wide with neighbors that have bears chained in the front yard, whiskey breath, and wearing yesterday's clothes. Of course, my cracker neighbors consume copious amounts of alcohol and are copulating around the clock, stopping only to eat, sleep and defecate. It is presumed the children of these folks are low functioning victims of fetal alcohol syndrome, parented by people who themselves need parenting. Seeing it as an opportunity to watch a full-blown stereotype in action, I play along.

"The world sure is different when you're looking at it from the heart of a trailer park," I'd tell them.

"You poor dear. . . are you afraid going home at night?"

"I don't go out after dark."

Beverly tried to comfort me, telling me it was only temporary and that "we're going to get you through this." She had a rather dim view of the world, and I think it came from her job as a forensic medical examiner for the city of NY. When not with her cadavers at work, she was on the 32nd floor of a high rise on third avenue with her cats, watching the lighted ribbons below and the traffic's constant flow.

"Do you need anything? I can send some dishes . . . and I have an extra set of pots."

"No, I have all that; furniture too. It's like staying in a rental, actually. The people I bought the house from left me with all that I needed to get started. Nice folks."

Beverly wasn't being mean in her attitudes towards Florida's less sophisticated residents. All she knew was what she saw on her monitors and phone. I was guilty of the same prejudice. When my kids were young and losing interest in their schoolwork, I would admonish them and try to instill in them a fear of living in a box set on cinderblocks, with broken steps, flanked by grease-covered barbeque grills. I painted a pretty scary picture of what it is like to be poor and that it was not an option.

"You'd better learn how to do something in this world, or you'll be standing in line waiting for handouts," I'd tell them, which worked until the last year of high school. By then, my tales of the 'great depression' drew chuckles and snide remarks. My son, who has always been adept at facetious sarcasm, when I told him of my move to Florida, asked me,

"Gee, dad is living in a trailer like what you told us when we were kids?" In my mind's eye, I could see his snarky smile, which I returned 'tout suite.'

"Well, . . . it's not like any place else I've ever lived before, I can tell ya that."

Alexey and I both enjoyed a verbal joust, and he was really good at it, something I was proud of. A chip off the old block, so to speak. But behind the banter, there was genuine concern,

"Don't worry, dad, we'll get ya out of there." But he just couldn't resist, "If you work hard and study, you won't ever have to live in a trailer again."

******

Malcolm is a filmmaker friend of mine living in Manhattan. High above the busy sidewalk, he watches humanity schooling along the canyons of the city. It fascinates him, my living in a trailer park, and he wants complete details about the people and the goings-on in the community. He's the kind of guy who rides the subway, so to be with the 'real people.' He'll get on the 'A' train and ride it to the end of the line. Then back again. Back and forth from 207th street to Far Rockaway until he has had his fill of the masses. He likes to visit the bodegas in the Bronx. While using the botanical gardens or little Italy as an excuse for travel, his true destination was the different shops in the area where he would hang out and play dominoes. Sometimes winning! The aromas, the ethnicity, and the society of people drew him back again and again. He said the atmosphere was intoxicating. I've always thought the aromas in the bodegas were from the overripe plantains and the yellowing chicken legs in the display case. A sure way to lose your appetite if you're trying to diet.

But I too, respected these good folks. The pictures displayed behind the counter showed their home and the work it took to move to the U.S. and open a business. Industrious and brave, they carved for themselves a niche in the great metropolis, and they were proud people.

"This place is not quite like you imagine Malcolm. Perhaps what you're looking for is true somewhere, but not here."

I told him we had two large lakes in the trailer park, well stocked with fish. Folks jump in their golf carts in the morning, drive to their favorite fishing spot, and start the day competing with the Osprey for the bass. Beginning at daybreak, cyclist circle the park, greeting friends and neighbors on their power walks. Anglers, cyclist, walkers' wave and bid each other good morning. The rabbits and squirrels chase each other about with abandon, without fear. The Sandhill cranes that walk along the shore stand about five feet tall. A verity of ducks stroll with the wood-stork and the ubiquitous Ibis's, avoiding the fast-moving squirrels as they forage. A large turtle warms himself on the pavement, collecting the energy to begin his day. Otters crawl and play on a log in the middle of the lake.

"And my favorite . . . is the Anhinga. This guy does his fishing underwater, and when he comes up for air, he looks like a miniature Loch Ness monster patrolling the lake. After swimming and filling his belly, he faces the sun, spreads his wings, and dries himself majestically, stating his 'I AM.'"

"Not exactly what I was hoping for!" complained Malcolm

"Well, wait, there's more. There is a large clubhouse here with a billiard room and a library. A café, work-out room, and event hall complete with a stage for shows. Outside, there is a full-size heated pool for use year-round. Bocce courts, shuffleboard, tennis courts —"

"You're boring meeee . . . what happened to the drunken orgies, the wife swapping and craziness. Tell me about someone hiding from the mob with pit bulls for pillows."

"So far, I've met retired military, teachers, small business owners, and such. Seems most people are living on their 401Ks, pensions, social security, and have enough disposable income to indulge themselves with retirement toys. It's the quietest place I've ever lived as well. It's an age-restricted community, fifty-five and older, so you're not getting the thump-thump of car radios at three in the morning. Lots of gray hairs but little noise."

I didn't like disappointing Malcolm, even felt a little bad for letting him down. But then I realized that although the ambiance of Lakeside Park was shire-like, the population, myself included, were all fucking weird. I don't know if it's the place that makes us that way or that everybody has always been weird, and I didn't bother to notice. The fact of the matter is that this is a fishbowl with a cavalcade of characters.

"Hold on, man, just hold on. There's more. We have it all here. Tattooed ladies galore. And I'm not talking about a rose discreetly placed on a shoulder. I'm talking tattoos that cover an entire arm or leg, sometimes with cryptic messages known only to the bearer. Tattoos that have faded and changed with the landscape of its canvass. We have handicapped people who ride motorcycles and scooters. For sure, there is a fair share of folks from the witness protection program or those released from the hospital with medication. I've heard stories about bordellos, and pot growers, and even a murder, though those people snuck in from outside to do a drug deal. Everyone is from somewhere else. Every accent in the country is spoken here, some which I don't understand."

"Ah . . . a Tower of Babel . . . that could be interesting."

"And a good number of them ride three-wheeled bicycles. What does that tell you?"

"That the residents of your shire ride around in chariots babbling incoherently?"

"Exactly!"

"But couldn't you scrounge up a meth lab somewhere in the trailer park?"

Malcolm had modest success years back with short films and a documentary on flesh-eating bacteria. He was always looking for new material and had a cadre of friends who he badgered for stories. I wouldn't be able to help him this time though. Yes, these people were covered in tattoos. They talked funny, drove yellow mustang convertibles, and pushed their dogs around in baby carriages, but they are also the people who worked the food banks. The folks who tutor kids in reading and math, who visit the elderly in their homes and in the hospital. These people are the salt of the earth, the ones who actually do something to make the world a better place. Not at all like our group in New York, whose expertise lie in complaining about life's inconveniences.

"I don't think there's anything here for you, Malcolm. But hey, I just got to Florida. Let's see how it works out. I'll let you know if I come across anything interesting."

After hanging up the phone, I realized it would make an interesting project to collect sketches of my neighbors and the goings-on in the park. Vignettes of our microcosm. It would take my mind off the lawyers and my divorce. We certainly are an eclectic group, and it would keep me busy. I may very well have my own little *Tortilla Flat* going here and should take advantage of it while I drift through the never-never land of the legal system. I would start with the cul-de-sac on which I live. Opening my laptop, I started a new word document calling it 'Thumbnails.' I entered the first name on my list.

Strange Day

Everything is quiet. As quiet as when the snow falls. Something strange is happening. Outside my window, the clouds weigh heavily upon the rooftops; close to the earth. There are no birds in the sky, no squirrels on the lawn; the rabbits have disappeared. I smell fear. The streets are deserted. Cars are parked haphazardly in an eerie disarray. My cat is hiding under the bed, the dog is whining in the corner. I am confused and off-balance.

The phone flashes wildly, demanding I read my messages. I don't want to. *I don't want to know.* Whatever it is, will have to wait until I get my bearings. *Coffee . . . you need coffee. Make some coffee and wake up.*

The coffee is hot and brings a reassuring warmth to my body. But it's not enough to quell the uneasiness that is running through my nervous system. Everything outside of my window is in grayscale. The crows have taken to the Holly tree across the street, turning it black, emitting a cacophony of screeches and caw, caw, caws. I butter a roll and return to the window, hoping the food will make it all go away, but it doesn't. The sun is higher in the sky but to no avail. No change in light or temperature. No activity from my neighbors. *Where did the wind go? Why do I feel this way? I had better turn on the television.*

The stations I have programmed on the remote only show snow with a grinding wall of static, making them unbearable. I hit the number one button and find a screen stating it is the **National Information Center** and that updates will be posted as they become available. The banner scrolling at the bottom of the screen declares that in order to conserve resources and to suppress dis-information, we have suspended all regular programming until further notice.

All right, all right . . . just tell me what the hell is going on? The screen is frozen, but the banner at the bottom continues with its message. Flicking through the channels, I find it is the only station working. *What the fuck is happening?* The phone is buzzing, telling me I've received new messages. *Maybe I can find out something there.* I hit the news icon, and it delivers the same message that is on the television.

"Stay tuned for updates from the National Information Center."

Maybe there's something in my voice mail?

"Daddy, this is Linda. I guess you know about what's happening. In case I don't get to speak to you later, I want you to know how much I love you and how grateful I am for having you as a Dad. Love you Daddy, hope we can talk later. Love ya!"

Love ya too, darling. Get back to you in a bit. Next message:

"Hello Phillip . . .this is your ex-wife. I am calling you to ask for forgiveness for any pain and suffering I might have caused you. This is long overdue, but better late than never. I want you to know I am working hard to make amends to the people I have harmed—"

Yah, yah . . . next.

"Hey Phillip, this is Mario, from Venice. How are you doing? I really want to know because everything here is weird. The canals are rising; the clouds are right over my head; I can't see the Cathedral. Everything is gray. The world has stopped. Not a soul in the Piazza. The pigeons are in hiding; there's no sun. What the hell is happening? How are things with you? I hope better. Call me if you hear what's going on. Addio Amici, Andare con Dio.

I still don't know anything about what's happening. All I know is that my daughter loves me; the ex is on step eight and Mario is in a cauldron. But what the hell is going on? I should go outside, see for myself.

I fill my travel mug with coffee and leave the house through the garage. Everything is still in gray scale; only now it's intensely surreal. The clouds sit atop the tall palms, making them look like tent poles. The air feels compressed, forced to earth by the heavy canopy. There is the smell of burning chemicals in the air. The cries of anguish creeping down the road send a shiver up my spine. People are shouting, crying, laughing hysterically. A dog runs frantically from between the houses, freezing when he sees me.

"It's Ok, boy . . . your OK."

The spell is broken, and the dog continues down the road, disoriented, tail between his legs and head hung low. There are shouts from across the lake. The Klabors are arguing loudly. Mrs. Klabor follows behind her husband, waving her arms in the air as they circle the house. Round and round as they argue, the sound fading in and out as they circumnavigate the house. The roar of a motorcycle grows louder as it approaches. A woman in a red ball gown is riding the bike. She has long blonde hair that flows behind her like a train. Periodically she shouts out a "YAH HOOOOH" I try to wave her down, hoping she would fill me in on what's going on. No such luck. She flies by. *She must be doing seventy miles an hour.* The dog returns . . . stops to eyeball me and moves on. He appears to be looking for something, moaning as he goes along.

Someone is walking up the road. *Finally! Someone to talk to. Thank goodness.* Hands behind his back, he is chanting OM .

. . Mani . . . Padme . . . OM. He is wearing a white shirt and pants. He has long black hair with a full beard. He looks like Allen Ginsberg. *It can't be Allen Ginsberg; he's been dead for years. Unless I'm dead too?*

As he gets closer, I see that it's not the Beat poet, and I am really glad.

"Hello, hello! Good to see ya." I said, running up to him.

"And hello to you. Good to see you too. How are things going?"

"I don't know. I don't know what the hell is going on. My TV is all snow, and my phone is useless."

"Wow, what are the chances of meeting someone who doesn't know what's going on? Walk with me; I'll fill you in. If I'm going to go the way of the dinosaur, I've got to keep moving forward, right till the end."

"Dinosaur . . . the end? What are you saying?"

"The last update from the National Information Center was at four-thirty this morning. Throughout the night, they were telling us a large asteroid was heading for the earth, but that most of it will have broken up by the time it reaches the earth's atmosphere. The damage close to the impact sight would be great, but most of the planet would be spared. Then early this morning, a spokeswoman came on and said that the asteroid was growing through accretion rather than breaking up and is expected to impact somewhere in the Pacific Ocean. That's the last we heard from them. They haven't got a clue. Everything that is happening is the opposite of what they expect it to be. I say, if this thing grows big enough, it could split the earth into a bunch of pieces. Then we'd have a bouquet of earths. It could change the whole dynamic of the solar system."

Instead of getting smaller, the fucking thing is growing in size.

And it's going to hit the earth!

"People are reacting in all kinds of ways. The churches are packed to capacity. Some folks are running around acting like paramilitary. People are walking into the ocean and not returning; suicides are common, you know, when paradigms radically shift."

"I'm sorry sir, but I have to go. I have some calls to make. Thank you for your help. All the best to you."

"Good luck with that. Best to look the monster in the eye, and that's what I aim to do."

Turning back to the house, I could feel the temperature rising, and I picked up my pace.

I should have called Linda right back. What was I thinking! Maybe we have time . . . .

FLASH!!!!!!

Erik's First Guitar

While riding my bike ride through the Shire one morning, I ran into Erik. He's a tall thin fellow with a salt and pepper crewcut, weathered face, and eye's that fix on you while he talks. Erik has a trunk full of stories he loves to tell, rambling and embellishing his world with incredible characters in off-beat situations. He is a comic and laughs at his own jokes. He has a Golden Retriever he calls Artemis[6]. Most folks in the shire have GMO[7] dogs—little dogs, some only ankle-high, nervous and hyper. You worry about stepping on them as they wrap their leash around your legs. Not Artemis, on or off the leash, she is well behaved. During my ride, I saw Artemis in the distance, picking up a newspaper in the driveway and sitting at the road's edge to wait for her owner to cross over with her. She delivered the newspaper to her neighbors' doorstep, tail wagging happily, and accepted the praise and petting from the man as they waited by the road for me to pass.

"Now that's a dog!" I said, and we made an immediate connection. The three of us.

Artemis was a dog you felt could understand what you were saying to her, answering with her body, laughing with her tail.

"That your bike over there?" I asked, pointing to a highly polished Harley in the driveway across the street.

"Yup . . . That's my baby. That's my number three."

---

[6] Artemis: Mother Goddess to the ancient Ephesians.
[7] GMO: Genetically modified organism.

"Number three?"

"Yup . . . My wife, my dog, my Harley and my guitars . . . in that order. That's what's important to me. A late model SUV pulled up, and a woman in her late fifties stepped out.

"That's my number one. Artemis here is number two, and my guitars are number four."

"You play guitar?"

"Since I've been 'bout fourteen. Still got my first guitar. But I mostly play my Fender Strat now. Had that since 1970."

"Really! . . . not many like that that around . . . you've got some six-string treasures there."

"You get the drift," laughing and putting out his hand, "The name is Erik . . . glad to meet ya."

"Walter . . . I live in #923, over on Sandpiper. I've seen you around, riding your bike."

"Yeah, sure. Frosty Samuels lives up the street from you. We're ridding buddies."

"So, what's the make of that first guitar you were talking about?"

"That's a story in itself."

Erik's wife calls out, reminding him they have an appointment at ten o'clock and that they didn't want to be late.

"Okay, Betty, I'll be right along. Walt, why don't ya drop by this evening, and we'll have a beer and shoot the breeze. I'll tell ya the story 'bout my first guitar."

"Sounds good; I'll drop by around seven." Patting Artemis on the head, I was off to finish my morning ride.

My daily bike routine is to circle the park, ride over to the mailboxes to pick up the mail; then it's back to the house to start the day's business. Takes about an hour. A routine that helps me clear the head and provides the only exercise I get during the day. After a bike ride and a shower, I'm ready for anything.

******

Erik and Betty's house is on the lake. Pastel blue, with white trim, the house is covered with bougainvillea growing on lattice, profusely flowered in purple and red. I rode over on my bike and found Erik straitening up the carport. We walked around back to a large deck that almost reached the water. They had the panoramic view. Ringed by colorful cottages with sleeping kayaks on the shore, all the activity of the lake lay before them.

"Beer-wine-Dr. Pepper, what's your pleasure?"

"I'll have a beer, thanks."

The Ibis gathered around the deck. Fishing poles stood at the ready, fastened to the corners. The ducks swam into the wind, creating a steady stream of ripples behind them. My host returned with the drinks.

"Plenty of birds on this side of the lake Erik; looks like they're all here."

"Lots of food and good hunting on this end. I get to watch the Osprey and the eagle do their thing as well."

We sat talking and watching the day slip away. I told him how I moved from NY and had reinvented myself as a writer.

"I stepped in shit when I found Vero Beach."

"I'll drink to that!" laughed Erik, raising his glass.

"So, what's the story with the guitar?"

"Oh, yeah . . . that's a good one. If you're a writer, you should write this one down."

He went on to say he grew up in an Irish neighborhood in St. Louis, Missouri. His dad had passed away a couple of years earlier, and his mom was still trying to get her bearings, now that she had to take care of everything by herself. He tells his story, staring out over the lake as though he were watching pictures drift by. "She managed . . . sometimes happily, sometimes chaotically. But she always did her best. Times were rough back then, and it was hard for her to relax. On the horizon, there was always an uncertain future awaiting us".

Betty brought a tray of munchies and joined us on the deck.

"Mom was pretty straightforward when she had something to say and came right to the point."

'Erik, I got another letter from your school. This time they want me to go down to the school for a meeting with the principle. Erik, what did you do?'

'I didn't do nothing'!'

"There's gotta' be a reason for the principle to want to speak with me. Did you get in a fight or something?"

"I ain't never been in a fight . . . at school that is. I passed all my tests, stayed out of trouble. I even took part in class discussions. There's only a couple of days left; I don't know what this is about."

"Maybe they're going to' give you a scholarship!"

"I doubt it Ma . . . I said I passed the tests . . . the scores weren't all that high . . . but high enough!"

"Maybe there's an award for that."

******

"Next morning, Mom and I went about our usual routine silently. Neither of us were morning people and really didn't come to life until after the third cup of coffee. Our appointment was for ten o'clock, so there was no need to hurry. Not to be too early, we waited as long as we could before leaving.

'Guess I won't be needing my book bag.'

'Probably not.'

We walked to the corner to catch the local #101 bus to the school. The June sun was already warming the air, and the trees were rushing to flower. The bus came, and we got on. I sat by the window while Mom filled the coin box. The streets were a lot busier than my usual trek earlier in the morning. Shopkeepers were opening their stores and sweeping the sidewalks. People hustled along the streets with a sense of urgency. We approached a row of stores I paid special attention to every day."

'Mom . . . remember you said at the beginning of September that if I got through the school year, you'd get me something special for a for a job well done?'

'I sure do, and I meant it'

'Well, I know what I want . . . See that pawn shop up ahead . . . check out the window when we pass. There, there, that guitar . . . that's what I want! I've passed by it every day since school began, watching and hoping nobody bought it.'

'It is a pretty one . . . not like the one's the rock and rollers play.'

'I looked it up at the library . . . it's for playing folk music and classical stuff.'

'Do you know how much it cost?'

'No.'

'Okay, we'll talk about it again after we take care of this business.'

The rest of the way to school, I imagined myself playing my new guitar to great accolades and thunderous applause. I was eager to get started.

Everyone was in class, so the hallways were empty. I was glad because I didn't want to have to explain why my mom was at school with me. I doubled my pace and headed straight for the principal's office, mom trying her best to keep up with me. When I reached the principles door, I waited so we could go in together. She was a little winded as she introduced herself to the secretary.

'Hello, I'm Emma Czerny, and this is my son Erik. We have an appointment to see the principle.'

'Of course, Mrs. Czerny. Please, have a seat. Hello Erik, I'll let monsignor Kelly know you're here, mam.'

"Oh, I forgot to mention Walt, it was a catholic school I went to. It was believed at the time that the catholic schools offered a better education, and though expensive, mom wanted me to have a good start in life. We had just sat down when the monsignor came out to greet us.

'Mrs. Czerny, so glad to meet you. Please, come into my office where we can talk.'

Monsignor Kelly had a big office with an enormous desk. Large leaded windows on one side of the room, bookshelves on the other. Behind his chair was a painting of Jesus suffering on the cross.

We all sat, and the Monsignor began.

'Mrs. Czerny, I am sorry to have to inform you we won't be accepting Erik back to Bishop Dubois H.S. next year. Issues have arisen over the past year concerning Erik's beliefs, especially in the area of religion. We feel it is causing a distraction to the rest of our students who are working hard, trying to learn the cannon of the church.'

'I don't know what you're talking about.'

'Erik seems to be quite taken with the religious groups in

the time of Jesus. Especially the Essene sect at Qumran, where the dead sea scrolls were found.'

'What scrolls? Erik, you never mentioned anything about scrolls to me.'

'I didn't think you'd be interested.'

'I'm glad he didn't learn this at home . . . I was going to recommend family counseling.'

'I don't understand! . . . there's nothing' to get frightened about. They're mostly the same books that are in the bible.' I said perhaps a little too loud.

'Not all of them . . . some have not been sanctioned by the church yet, the monsignor said, raising his voice above mine.

'So now you can include them. Maybe it was a mistake leaving them out!'

'It is not your place to determine church cannon, young man. Enough! . . . and Mrs. Czerny, then there's the matter of tuition. You are behind six months.'

'I will have that cleared up very soon, monsignor. Certainly, before school starts in the fall. Right now, I'm borrowing from Peter to pay Paul.'

'Yes, I know your story, and you are a courageous woman for all you do, but we at Bishop Dubois have bills and responsibilities just as you do, and tuition pays the bills. Surely you understand, Mrs. Czerny. You expect to be paid for your work, and so do we. I'm sorry, but we have already given Erik's place to a new applicant.'

'Okay . . . that ends that.' Mom said, standing. 'Please send Erik's report card to the house, and we thank you for your time Monsignor. Erik, time to go!'

She was out the door and flew through the reception room before another word could be said. I had to hustle to keep up with her as she barreled down the hallway. By the time we reached the exit, the classroom doors opened, and the kids flooded the corridors on the way to their next class. We made it outside without being seen. I was glad, even though I was being kicked out of school, and it didn't matter. We sat in the bus stop kiosk to wait for the next bus.

'You did nothing wrong, Erik. It's their problem, not yours. I'm proud of you for studying something on your own and giving them a run for their money. What's in these scrolls that gets them so upset?'

'They just started translating them, but it looks like they are really old versions of the books that are in the bible, and a couple of new ones they didn't know existed. I read about them in the archaeology magazines at the library. The Catholic scholars are afraid it will contradict church cannon and want to control the translations and its release. The Jewish scholars pitch a fit and get involved, claiming the scrolls as their own. A big fight is going on.'

'You're right. I'm not interested.'

We got on the bus and sat solemnly, waiting to leave. I sat on the side where the pawnshop would be, as I did every day. There was no air-conditioning in the busses in those days, so all the windows were open. The noise from the street and the bus engine created a din that you had to talk over. Mom took my hand and smiled to console me.

'Mom, honest, it's no big deal. I really don't care. I'm glad I don't have to go back to that school. They're a bunch of dummkopfs . . . who needs them?'

'Where do you learn this stuff?'

'The library.'

The pawn shop was coming up, so I turned my attention back to the window. The guitar was still there, and I wondered if I would ever see it again, seeing as I would not be attending Bishop Dubois H.S. anymore. Mom jumped up out of her seat,

'Erik, pull the stop cord; we're getting off,' and walked to the rear doors, 'We're going to make some lemonade!'

The doors of the bus opened to the entrance of the pawnshop. We strolled in, not changing a step. The shop was empty. No one behind the counter, no sales personnel. The antiques throughout the store seemed to beckon us, all wanting to speak at the same time. Everything you could imagine was there, and some things you may have never dreamed of as well. The guitar in the window set off an amber glow. A stout, bearded man opened a curtain and greeted us.

'Good morning. How can we help you today?'

'We're interested in that guitar in the window.' Mom said, trying to sound businesslike.

'What are you asking for it?'

'We've had that guitar for quite a while . . . So long, it's become part of the decor. I can give it to you for . . . twenty-eight dollars, he said, walking over to fetch the guitar. On the way back to the counter, he stared me in the eye and said that he knew I would make a suitable home for the 'red-head'. Turning to my mom, he told her, 'Mrs. Czerny, since I don't have the documentation and there are no labels on the guitar, I can let you have it for twenty-two fifty. There are no labels or paperwork, but! . . . Son, come over here, take a look.'

Looking into the body of the guitar, I could see initials J.H.T. carved on the back.

'It could come in handy someday.' He said.

He was right. Years later I found out that the guitar was made by a master luthier in Seville, Spain. It was his personal guitar.

We left and waited at the bus stop. I felt very proud carrying my guitar case, and mom looked proud too. Taking our seats, I looked out of the open window to see the pawnbroker standing in his doorway.

'Mom, how did he know your name was Mrs. Czerny?

'I don't know. I didn't tell him, . . . and I paid cash money. That guy was kind of weird, so best not to know what he's about.'

******

When we got home, I spent the rest of the day polishing and familiarizing myself with my new treasure. There was a new set of strings in the guitar case. Nylon with gold bass strings, and when strung, the guitar sounded deep and mellow, with bright, rich tones. I got up early and went to the library as soon as it opened. I found a book on how to "Teach yourself to play the guitar in ten easy lessons." Another one on how to read music, and one on music theory. I've been studying ever since."

"So, you taught yourself how to play?"

" I teach myself everything. Always have."

"That is a good story, Erik."

"I've got a million of them!"

"Well, I should head out . . . my cat is a demanding mistress and pouts when she's not fed on time."

"I know the feeling. Drop by again sometime, and I'll tell ya the story about how I got the Fender. I won it in a card game. Won it, lost it, and won it back again. It was a wild night."

"Will do. Thank you both for everything."

They both wished me a good night and walked me to the

front of the house. I jumped on my mountain bike and headed home. The shire looked like the set of a Disney movie, with all the cottages lit up and the colored glow from the televisions flashing like strobe lights. The moon was rising and looked very heavy as the clouds drifted by it. When I opened the door, the cat gave me a growl, sat in front of her bowl, and waited to be fed. I gave her a can of Friskies, got myself a beer, and sat down at the computer to make notes on the newest addition to the cast of characters that peopled the Shire.

The Night Misha was Born

Serge handed me a blood-soaked bundle, wrapped in a blanket. He searched my eyes to see that I knew what I had to do. I nodded and left. I carried it to a place already agreed upon. Atop of a hill overlooking the house, we had dug a pit beside a healthy sapling. A walnut tree that would one day shade the house from the unforgiving summer sun. Walnut trees are well adapted to the region, and this one, planted only two months earlier, was flourishing. Like a supplicant carrying an offering, I negotiated the bundle up the steep hill. I placed my precious cargo beside the sapling and got down on my knees to examine the pit. After scooping out a few handfuls of dirt that had fallen in, I sat back on my haunches, stared at the sapling, then at the bundle, and turned my eyes to the sky. We had dug the pit deep enough so that the wild animals could not pick up the scent of the flesh below. Hopefully, they would pass by and leave the grave alone. It was close enough to the house where Serge and Dahlia could keep an eye on it; looking for depressions in the landscape or signs of scavengers.

We had discussed everything, planning thoroughly each step, down to the smallest detail. I felt detached like I was going through the motions of a well-rehearsed drama. My mind tried to order the chain of events and their meanings. It all took on a ritual-like importance. I was a participant, a prop in a cosmic event. An x-ray collage of episodes being recorded in the dark matter of what is. I closed my eyes and relived everything that had taken place.

I drove up to the ranch from San Francisco in my old Karmen Ghia. It would be a risky trip as the VW needed work, and I hadn't been able to put the money together for the repairs yet. I had been coddling and nursing it for over a month. Whenever possible, it was the bus, trolley, or hitchhiking when moving about San Francisco. The Karmen Ghia was a stick shift, and I was having problems with second gear. I had to push first gear to the max, then slide past second and into third. It's amazing how attuned one could become to their car. Listening to its engine speak, or the transmission clanking, was like getting to know a person. In a city of hills with too many stoplights, it was best to leave the Ghia at home. But to where I was going, being without a car was not an option, so I went for it.

It was a little tricky getting on the freeway. I had to wait for the entrance lane to be completely clear before I ventured out, much to the chagrin of those behind me. Once on the highway and in third gear, we were good to go. It was a three-hour drive to Serge and Dahlia's place from the city. After I drove over the Bay Bridge, past El Cerrito and Richmond, the rest of the way would be clear sailing. I would take the right-hand lane through the rolling hills, right to Grass Valley. The road climbed steadily on its trek to Lake Tahoe and the Sierra Nevada Mountains. It had rained for a couple of days, so the hills were green with new growth and fresh wildflowers in full bloom. Cattle grazed, feasting on the new shoots brought by the rains. Most of the year, the hills were a golden tan color, so this was an unexpected perk on the drive.

Vacaville-Davis-Sacramento flew by with little traffic and

no detours. The last leg of the journey was to Grass Valley, where I would turn off and take the county roads to Serge and Dahlia's place. They lived in the foothills; eight miles up a winding forested road, crossing rivers and streams through the unpredictable hills. This land was only hospitable to those willing to claim it and make it their own; the people who put in the work to tame it.

When I drove up the cut-off to the house, I saw Serge in the fields herding the sheep towards the barn. He waved, and I pulled over and parked.

"Boy, am I glad to see you!" he said, giving me a big hug. "I've been swamped here and sure could use a hand."

"And here I am! How's Dahlia?"

"She's good; everything's coming along . . . First thing I need you to do is run to town and pick up some cleaning supplies. You get the Ghia fixed?"

"No, not yet. But it's good. She hummed all the way here."

"Take the pickup . . . here are the keys. I should be through by the time you get back, and we can talk then. Andy, I gotta' get the sheep to the barn for the shear man in the morning. Thanks for coming buddy, we'll talk later."

I drove up to the house and stopped in to say hi to Dahlia but didn't see her. If she was resting, I didn't want to disturb her, so I went on my way. The pickup truck was a pleasure to drive. All eight cylinders firing perfectly, and it handled like a sports car. Shiny, new, waxed, it would have been great for low-riding main street in Grass Valley; if I didn't have other things to do.

The Safeway was crowded with shoppers. It was the largest food store in the area and was always busy. As usual, whenever we shopped there, someone was assigned to follow us around to make sure we didn't shoplift anything. For the management: long hair meant thief. It was fine with me. I had fun with it. I would make the person accompanying me my shopping assistant.

"Can you tell me where to find the Pate? . . . and the Camembert cheese . . . Oh yeah, and baguettes too."

"We only got white and yellow cheese, . . . What's Pate?"

"Fine . . . okay. Where's the cleaning stuff and the paper towels?"

He or she would lead me through the aisles to find all the items on my list. People stared at my cart, loaded with gallons of bleach, Lysol, and paper towels. I threw in a bag of chips and a soda in to make it look right.

"Sure, you got enough bleach?" chided the check-out girl, chuckling along with the bagger.

"I'm good, thank you." I paid and was escorted to the door. They watched me as I loaded the truck. Pickup trucks were a real status symbol in this part of California, and I had a shiny new one. I waved goodbye and headed back to the ranch.

******

When I got back to the house, Dahlia was there, moving about the kitchen, going about her business like she had a thousand times before. Big as a house, she would sit for a while, then return to her stove. She put the lid on the casserole dish and set it in the oven. Sitting down with a sigh, she told Serge,

"I think I should lie down."

He took her by the elbow and led her to the bedroom.

"Andy, take the tamale pie out of the oven in thirty-minutes," she said, walking slowly and deliberately, "thanks for coming to help Andy. I'll see you later."

This would be Serge and Dahlia's third child. Jewel, Patrick, and now Misha. All three were born at home, with Serge being the midwife. Except in Ireland, where Patrick was born. A state-licensed midwife was required on the Emerald Isle, and so Patrick had the two of them to help him with his entrance into the world. The woman was amenable. Let them do their thing and only assisted now and then. Serge and Dahlia said she was a little taken aback by working with a male midwife; not a popular occupational choice for men folk in Ireland.

I was flattered at first when they asked me to help. They had a lot of friends who they could have asked, some of whom had delivered their own babies at home. Our group of friends were an eclectic hodgepodge of personalities. Some were enlightened, being self-proclaimed experts on Eastern Religion, while others thought LSD was the breakfast of champions. Most were of the "back to basic's" school, and the Whole Earth Catalogue was their writ of common knowledge. All people with good hearts and a lot more experienced than I had.

It's because you're reliable and stay cool under pressure, I told myself.

Serge was a tall fellow. You were always looking up when talking with him. With bushy black hair and a full beard, he looked the part of the mountain man he was. Gregarious and good-natured, he made everyone feel at home. Dahlia was a petite girl with a winning smile and the long straight hair so common in the day. She was an intellectual, spiritual, erudite, and creative girl, with strong opinions, which she loved to share.

Everything was about the children. Piaget, Montessori, Rudolf Steiner, and of course Dr. Spock were all studied in the hope they might reveal some insight into the formation of a young mind and spirit. Their food was grown organically. The farm animals were free-range and only ate the best feed themselves. A great amount of attention was paid to the cooking, and Adel Davis's cookbooks were followed religiously. No drugs were consumed, including proscribed pharmaceuticals, and they only drank wine on gatherings and special occasions.

They loved to tell stories about the good ole days (they were only twenty-five years old) in San Francisco and Berkeley before the media descended on Haight-Ashbury. There was a constant flow of people between North Beach and Greenwich Village, and Serge was a legend on both sides of the country. Much of the mythology was created by Serge himself for a hungry audience that wanted to believe the adventures of an unconventional poet. Dahlia wrote poetry and children's books with guided spiritual messages. She corresponded with other poets and authors, the likes of Gary Snyder and Henry Miller, who encouraged her to keep working on her craft.

Serge grew up in a blue-collar neighborhood in Queens, New York, where everyone was enjoying the post-war boom and saving their money to move to Long Island. The schools were disciplined and presented a solid curriculum of studies in which Serge excelled. That is until he read Jack London and decided to emulate the author's lifestyle. Dahlia grew up in Berkeley California, where her parents both worked at the university. Her father worked at the research center, compiling sociological statistics, and her mom was a professor of Freudian psychology. Dahlia was a precocious child with an insatiable appetite for the new and the exotic. She met Serge at a poetry reading at the Fat Black Pussycat, a café in North Beach, and it was Kismet from the start. They merged and passed through each other, forming an aggregate of their personas, intertwining physically and spiritually like a caduceus. Like peanut butter and jelly.

******

Dahlia had made a great tamale pie. We each had two large helpings and an animated discussion about early cave art. Dahlia called it a day and said goodnight.

"I'll be right along, Dahlia," Serge said, stretching and yawning, then burping.

"Take your time. I'm going to take my tea and read myself to sleep. Good night, Andy."

"Night Dahlia."

Serge got right to business, "Looks like it will be a quiet night." Another burp from south of the border interrupted him, and like a migrant, it traveled across the room. "Anyways . . . everything is ready. Jewel and Patrick will be with the Greyson's until the end of the week, and we have all the supplies we will be needing. The pots for the boiling water are on the stove, ready to go. There is a list of phone numbers and addresses on the refrigerator door. In the laundry room are the fresh towels and blankets we will be needing."

"What are the newspapers for?" I said, pointing to a stack of Sunday New York Times by the bedroom door.

"The closest were going to get too sterile are these unopened newspapers. Could come in handy in a number of ways, so we have plenty on hand. I'm going to stay close to the house, so you'll have to let the sheep and cattle out to pasture in the morning and feed the chickens. I'll take care of breakfast. Oh yeah, the shear man will be coming early to shear the sheep in the corral. Did I tell you not to let them out with the others? Well, don't, cause he's a pain in the ass to get to come out here, and I don't want him giving me any excuses about why the sheep haven't been shorn. And, if we get the chance, I'd like to work on the barnyard gate, its sagging pretty bad and dragging on the ground. I know it sounds like a lot, but it's really not. Just another day, actually." He gave me a hug.

"Thank you, buddy. When it comes your time, I'll be right there with you."

"Goodnight, Serge."

******

I didn't want to admit it to myself, but I was scared shitless. When we talked about birthing children at home, it was always as a story. Something I could boast about and be proud that my courageous and independent friends were living life on their own terms. But this was the real thing. I didn't know what to expect. Suppose something went wrong, what then? The nearest doctor and hospital were eight miles away in Grass Valley. It wasn't the distance that was the problem; it was the winding road through the foothills that took all the time. I looked at the big pots on the stove and the stack of newspapers by the door, wondering what the hell I got myself into. I was fine with throwing the animals a bale of hay, filling the water troughs, feeding the chickens, fixing whatever needed fixing. I had seen the sheep birthing their lambs, helped Bessie the dairy cow drop her calf. I played Vet to the Angus and their young. It was kind of messy, but all part of the cycle of life. This was different. This was Dahlia. It seemed so risky for her to walk the fine line between life and death just because it was natural. Even in hospitals, with doctors and nurses and all their equipment, things could go wrong. We were literally in the wilderness and only had ourselves to rely on. It seemed to me, considering what was at stake, it would be best to get all the help one could get. I was tired and was ready for bed. It had been a long day, and I had an early start in the morning.

******

I awoke early. The moment I opened my eyes, I was fully charged and ready to go. The coffee on the stove had finished percolating and its aroma filled the kitchen. Serge was not around, but I could hear murmurs from the bedroom.

"Breath in . . . that's it . . . breath out . . .and again!"

There was a bowl of fruit on the table, butter and rolls on the cutting board, and the coffee was piping hot. I helped myself to the fresh bread and two perfectly ripe peaches. It was a good start to the day.

The cattle and sheep were waiting impatiently, making a ruckus, yelling for me to open the gate to the pasture. Sheep are especially cranky in the morning. I had a problem with a mean-spirited ram that had butted me several times from behind when he was unsatisfied with my job performance. I was ready for the ram that morning. Like a bull fighter spreading his cape, I opened the gate, and the ram charged through. He turned, kicking the dirt, snorting to let me know he was in charge. He joined the flock, prancing around, bellowing about his prowess. Fine with me. A ram enamored with himself will make happy ewes, which will make big healthy lambs.

I fed the chickens and prepared the shear pen. I swept and hosed it down, gathered the burlap bags for the shorn wool, and made everything ready. The shear man Jenkins arrived late, smelling of whiskey, and was half toasted. He needed a shave and looked like he had slept in his clothes. The sheep didn't react very well to him either, scurrying off into the corners of the corral when he entered. Tom, the barn cat, sat on a fence post at the far end, watching. I didn't blame them. I was uncomfortable being around the guy myself. He talked a lot, and when he spoke the few remaining teeth he had forced you to turn your head in disgust. They were stained from the chewing tobacco he was constantly gnawing on. He spit out the tobacco juice at regular intervals, some of it landing on his shirt. The guy was a mess. But as inebriated as he was, he went about his work efficiently and methodically. We collected six bags of wool.

When I got back to the house, Serge was making French toast. Coltrane was on the record player, and Dahlia was talking away about the names she was considering for the new baby. She looked perky and refreshed, discussing the effects different names would have on people throughout their lives. She was leaning toward the Russian. Serge wanted a French name, especially if it was a girl. I stayed out of it, enjoying their banter. Some of the names they came up with would certainly make an impression. When the 'what if's' and 'could-be's' were added to the conversation, it became wildly comical, and we all had a good belly laugh. They decided it that if it were a boy, Dahlia would name him and if a girl, Serge would choose.

Afterward, Dahlia went to her room to write, and Serge and I started on the repairs of the barnyard gate. Earlier, he had installed an eyelet and a stainless-steel cable to the tall fence post at the back end. It was a long gate, so gravity had had its way with it. I held up the front end while Serge ratcheted the cable taut, allowing it to swing freely; just high enough that the chickens could pass underneath. We made short work of that project and were off to our burial site.

We grabbed a couple of shovels and made our way up the hill. I could see the kitchen window from where we were digging. The sun had not baked the ground yet, so it was an easy dig. We worked carefully so not to disturb any of the roots of the newly planted walnut sapling. We dug the pit two-foot square and two-foot deep. As we worked, Serge told me that Dahlia was obsessing about the placenta and the respect she thought it deserved.

"She's writing an article about it right now. She's going to send it to the op-ed editors of all the newspapers."

Evidently, Dahlia felt it was an extremely important three-way relationship between the mother, the fetus, and the placenta. They were in constant contact, 24/7, informing each other of what needed to be done to produce a healthy baby. A nine-month-long conversation. A closeness and a bond like no other. To discard it with the trash after working so closely for so long seemed completely callous to her. In the op-ed, she suggested the placenta should be treated with gratitude and respect and that a ritual should be performed for its disposal as a part of the birth process.

"I actually agree with her," Serge said while digging. "It's like having this super nurse, who after devoting herself completely to her job, you throw her out when she's done. Not a good start. It wouldn't hurt to have a little ritual showing some respect for this miracle called life. Dahlia wants to start 'The Placenta League', you know, like the 'Le

Leche League'? She's going to appeal to celebrities and ask them to help make it fashionable."

"I, . . . I know nothing about this stuff . . . It's never come up before." I was completely caught off guard, "that's going to be quite an op-ed piece!"

"Yep . . . that's my Dahlia. What the hell? . . .showing a little respect can't hurt."

"No, it can't." It was all too deep for me, but what the hell.

When we finished, Serge left to go back to the house, and I went to hang out with the barn cat. Tom was huge. There was plenty for him to eat, so he grew to be the size of a bobcat. He was not your touchy-feely kind of cat. He kept his distance, observing from strategically located perches throughout the barn and the yard. He was aware of everything going on in his domain. Over time we became friends, and he followed me around during the day while I did my chores. I enjoyed his company as well. There was something special about his solitary nature, his confidence, and his acumen. We grew comfortable 'being there' together and sought each other's company whenever I visited.

When the sheep saw me open the gate to the corral, they ran down the hill in a frenzy. Their bells were ringing like crazy as they ran. Baaha-baaha, they bellowed in anticipation of the alfalfa hay and fresh water that was waiting for them. Serge and Dahlia had put bells around the necks of the sheep as a defense against coyotes and the big cats. If we heard those bells ringing at night, we'd grab a rifle and run to the barn to chase whatever was out there back into the hills. Didn't always work. There were mornings when Serge and Dahlia would find a half-eaten carcass, belly up, ravaged during the night. Sheep are strange. They will just stand and watch their young being eaten. Things had been getting better, and there had been fewer kills since they got the dog. But dogs and the bells can only do so much.

The cattle followed the sheep into the corral, and everyone was in for the night. Serge came by to give me a hand cleaning up the barn and putting everything away. We closed the doors and the gates and left for the house.

"I just have to stop in the garden and get the veggies I picked."

"Wow, vegetables this early?"

"We started them inside."

We opened the kitchen door to the smell of roast lamb finishing in the oven. Dahlia was waddling about, humming while setting the table.

"Oh good, you have the veggies. It's our first salad of the year!"

"I'll clean them up," Serge said, taking the basket to the sink. "You sit; I've got it."

"The roast will be ready in ten minutes. There are some red potatoes in the oven too. The lamb is a little heavy for us," she said, rubbing her belly, "I think we're going to have some chicken soup and a salad. . . . So, Andy, how's been your day?"

"Good Dahlia. Busy! It's amazing how much work gets done around here in a day. The roast smells great. How are you doing? Any predictions on the due date?"

"Soon, says the sparrow," pointing to the sky, "before the next moon! . . . geez, how do I know? I've been wrong so many times I don't trust my predictions anymore. When everyone's ready, we'll be good to go."

"You looked like Madam Blavatsky just then." Serge said, tossing the salad.

"In answer to your question, Andy . . . No. But soon!"

The dinner was superb. I jumped into the role of 'waiter', telling them I needed the practice.

"I have a job interview coming up in the city."

Afterward, we listened to jazz, played poker, and drank chamomile tea until everyone said they were tired and ready for bed. I took a shower and fell asleep reading.

******

I heard screams of pain. The door burst open with Serge yelling,

"Showtime!"

Running back, he called out, "Breathe Dahlia, breathe." I jumped out of bed, put my jeans on, and ran to the kitchen. I fired up the stove, filled the pots with water, and made the coffee. Clearing the table, I laid out the towels and blankets. I had decided on my own to have the truck ready to go should we need it. I ran outside to back it up to the house. I didn't have shoes on, and my feet were cold in the wet grass. I backed the truck up and ran back inside. The tea kettle was whistling, and the coffee pot perked.

Aw shit . . . I forgot the Bach!

I ran to the record player and put on the Brandenburg concertos.

Maybe I should have started with the Italian concerto . . . No, the partitas . . . Nah, the Brandenburg concertos are fine.

I went back to the kitchen, sat at the table, hands clasped, and asked myself,

Now what? . . . Guess you'll just have to wait and see.

At first, the screams from behind the door were intermittent. Equal amounts of downtime interspersed with primal cries of anguish. I never dreamed Dahlia, who was a small-framed girl, could ever evoke such volume and intensity. She sounded like a wild animal screaming at the universe. Sometimes defiantly, sometimes pleading. In between, there would be laughter. Serge was a comic with a witty sense of humor and always made Dahlia laugh. The laughter was good to hear but gave a manic feel to all that was going on.

I kept the tea kettle and coffee pot warm and changed the records on the record player. Occasionally Serge would pop his head out and make a request.

"Andy, find me something—fast-slow-fast-slow. Like a piano concerto or a light symphony or something. Start it at," looking at his watch "exactly 11:29. That should put us in sync. Breathe Dahlia, breathe," and he'd disappear behind the door. I was getting antsy sitting at the table, waiting for the next time the bedroom door opened. *This is going to be a long night; I should find something to do.* I went to the living room to find a book or magazine to read.

'The First Nine Months of Life' was sitting on the cocktail table. Seemed appropriate. It was a profusely illustrated book, so it would make for an easy perusal.

With a refill of coffee, I sat down on the couch to catch up on the beginnings of life. It turned out that most of what I knew about the entire process was the sex part; it's taking a lifetime to figure that out. The book blew me away. The coordination and synchronization from the big bang to completion, from a zygote to a person, was incredible

How did everything get so smart?

Made me feel dumb. All this has been going on around me, and I was clueless.

What else is going on that I don't know about?

The next book was a homemade version of the 'First Nine Months' Dahlia had worked on with the kids. It was made to be understood by a two- and five-year-old. It was as good as the big version, cute, with lots of pictures and cut out letters with sparkles. It covered everything from mommy and daddy kissing to holding baby after being born. It was a good read.

Judging from what I had just learned reading the kid's books, we were between major contractions. It had been quiet for a while, so I played some Wes Montgomery. Smooth L.A. guitar jazz seemed a fitting intermezzo between contractions. I even dozed off. Occasionally there would be screams. I could hear Serge's full voice, "Let it out, baby, give it to me!"

"You did this to me . . . it's all your fault."

"Well, stop being so dam good-looking! . . . breath Dahlia breath."

It was like they were singing a duet together. Everything seemed fine. I put on some Vivaldi and dozed off again until Serge burst into the room,

"Andy, she wants Bolero . . . Ravels Bolero. Start it at," looking at his watch . . . "4:32 . . . keep on playing it till I tell ya to stop. Gotta go!"

It took two renditions of Bolero to bring Misha into the world. At the end of the second take, I could hear Misha's contribution to the ensemble. They were now a trio. The three of them were whooping it up, singing, laughing, and crying for all the world to hear.

******

Serge came out of the room beaming.

"We have a baby-boy! And he's a big one. Must be eight

pounds! You can stop the music now . . . could ya make some fresh mint tea Andy? Time to celebrate."

"Sure. How's Dahlia?"

"She's doing good. She's glad that it's over. Looks like we're gonna' have a Misha in the family. Maybe next time, I'll get my Annette."

"They're both wonderful names."

"Great names for great people! I'm going to start cleaning up now, so keep the water hot and the towels coming. I'll be back," he said, disappearing behind the door.

I filled the kettle and made a fresh pot of coffee. A bowl of hot water and towels stood ready on a table by the door. *I should put some food together. They're bound to be hungry after all that.* But I couldn't cook. The burners were all being used. Misha was good; he had Dahlia. . . . *Dahlia will probably want something soft.* I cut up bananas, strawberries, peaches and found some yogurt in the fridge. I sliced apples and hard salami for Serge. French bread, Brie, and hot tea tied it all together. *Wait! something sweet.* I found some chocolate chip cookies in a jar on the counter, still soft. My make-shift fare was complete, and it looked great! I ate the roast lamb from the night before, cold, with some French bread and black coffee.

Serge popped out and took the bowl of water and towels back into the room. He came right back out, asking if the tea was ready. He was wide-eyed when he saw the food tray waiting for him and kept repeating:

"Brilliant! Absolutely brilliant! Yes, this is wonderful, absolutely," laughing as he disappeared into the room. "Look what I've got!"

I filled another bowl with boiling water, put fresh towels on the table, and went back to my roast lamb. All was good.

That's when Serge came out with a bloody bundle, wrapped in a blanket.

******

The sun hadn't reached the horizon yet. Slowly, everything became hyper-clear in the crisp, cool morning air. The local critters looked surprised and taken aback to find someone in the meadow so early. After all that examination, I couldn't say what force brought me to this place. I picked up the bundle and set it in front of me. After unwrapping the blanket, carefully folding back the towels — there it was. The placenta. It was the shape of a kidney bean, opaque yet translucent. Serge had neatly wrapped the umbilical cord around the edges, giving it a border. Looking at the placenta was like looking into the milky way. It had clusters of nerve endings, veins, and arteries that spread like the branches and roots of a tree. It looked almost alien, like a command pod from another galaxy. An incredible work of creation. A factory that converts nutrients and oxygen into a form the baby can absorb. *Who's in charge here?*

******

The shower was right next to Serge and Dahlia's bedroom, and I didn't want to disturb them, so I stopped in the laundry room and scrubbed my hands and face with lava soap. I went straight to my room, changed my clothes, and made ready to resume my duties. The water was on a low boil, the coffee hot, and the tea warm. All was quiet inside the room, and guessing that they were taking a nap, I drifted off myself. That is until Misha let out a howl. He was only a couple of hours old but could roar like a mountain lion, and that's what he did. It must have been a real shocker for him to leave Dahlia's warm amniotic fluid for the constant change of the outside world. And Misha was not shy in expressing his opinion of his new environment. It was almost like he was yelling, "What the fuckkkkk!" And then he'd go quiet. I assumed he was being fed.

Someday I'm going to tell this kid about all this!

******

The next morning, I awoke to the sound of Serge cooking in the kitchen. Sausage was crackling in the frying pan, and the scrambled eggs were being whipped in a bowl. The *ping-ping-flop-plop* of the mixture held a lot of promise and made me hungry. The coffee smelled great, and I caught a whiff of biscuits. There must be caffeine in the aroma of coffee because, at the urging of the olfactory, I was immediately awake and fully alert. Getting up from the couch, still dressed, I followed my nose. *Not a bad way to start the day.*

"Well, good morning Andy! Come sit down. Everything's just about ready."

"Smells great man . . . How's Dahlia and Misha?"

"They're both sleeping. Everything looks good though. Dahlia's doctor is going to come by later for a check-up to make sure. Good guy, this doctor, very supportive." Bringing my breakfast plate, he sat across from me with a cup of coffee. "Enjoy, Andy."

"You're not having any breakfast?"

"Nah, I'll wait for Dahlia; you go ahead." He leaned back in his chair, drinking his coffee. "As if you haven't done enough, we still have stuff to do. Today we've got to separate the shorn sheep from the unshorn ones. I need to get the shear guy back here so we can be done with that. I've called the Vet for Bossie cow too. I think she's ready to make us another bull-calf. But I'll take care of it. I have the sire all picked out. Other than that, it's the usual routine. I'll come out and help ya when I can, but I need to be close to Dahlia and the baby. . . . Even though they'll be sleeping most of the day, I still want to be within earshot."

"You want the sheep in the corral or in the nighttime pasture?"

"In the corral, that way we can usher them into the shearing pens when the Jenkins comes. Put the rest in the night pasture. . . . More coffee?" He poured the coffee while he told me the game plan. "The Greyson's are bringing the kids back home tomorrow. They're very excited and want to meet their baby brother. Then we can start getting back to normal. Dahlia's parents are driving up from Berkeley on Saturday, so be prepared for a full house with lots of traffic." Dahlia called from the bedroom, and Serge left. I finished my breakfast, did the dishes, then went to the barn to get started.

Tom, the barn cat, greeted me as usual, and we went to work. We opened the barn doors and windows to air it out. We turned the cattle out to pasture and fed the chickens. Turning the sheep out took a lot longer than usual. I had to let the shorn sheep out one or two at a time to prevent a stampede of the shorn and unshorn. They were not co-operative, and it was slow going. Amongst the unshorn was the nasty tempered ram. I was looking forward to this one getting a haircut. It would bring the bastard down a notch or two. Sheep always look funny after being shorn, and they look like they know it. Like they've been caught in their underwear or something. I threw them a half bale of hay to calm them down before their beauty parlor appointment.

The remaining sheep and the cattle followed Tom and I out into the pasture to fill the water troughs. They nudged and pushed each other out of the way, jockeying for position in front of the tub as it filled. More from routine than thirst as they had water in the nighttime pasture as well. I saw the shear-man parked at the barn, and I waved to let him know I would be right there. He was a half-hour early. I almost didn't recognize him. This was a changed man. He was clean-shaven, wearing a pressed shirt, new jeans, and polished cowboy boots. His truck was cleaned up as well. A complete transformation. He said he had put devil behind him and had turned to the Lord. I asked him to shear the nasty ram first in some kind of petty revenge for butting me the day before. Big horns, big head with a skinny little body; didn't look like no big shot now. I guess I was as big a jerk as he was. We finished in good time, and we had eight bags of wool. He said he had a prayer meeting in town and didn't want to be rude, but he had to go. He even invited us to his church.

Serge came to the barn with the Vet, discussing bull sperm.

"Well, is this Sire still producing?" Serge asked.

"Yeah . . . there just a little backed up right now. There's a lot of demand for this Sire, and it would be about a week before we can get a sample."

"I think I'll wait then. We've had excellent results with this bull, and I think I'll stay with him."

"Sounds good. I'll be back in a week, and we'll get Bossie all fixed up. She's in good shape and should make a great calf."

Serge and I walked back to the house, joking about how his life has changed.

"Not bad for a kid from Queens," Serge said proudly.

The Greyson's had arrived, and the kids were playing in the front yard. They gave me a big hug, saying they missed me and that I have to come stay with them. They were great kids. Dahlia was in the kitchen holding little Misha, chatting with her friend Grace. *I'm finally going to meet Misha.* He actually had hair. Blonde hair. A flaxen little Viking, long and lanky, with big gray eyes. *How could someone so little make so much noise?*

"Hello, little man, I've heard a lot about you. Heard your first song too. Glad to meet ya!"

Dahlia offered to let me hold him, but I refused, lacking the confidence to safely hold the little guy. Feeling like a klutz, I could not take responsibility for something so fragile.

The Greyson's had brought a stack of Pizzas, and after spending the day together, we all sat down to piazza and a salad. Both Dahlia and Grace were breastfeeding, and they would take turns whipping out the tit to feed the little ones. Serge and Jeff Grayson didn't notice at all, yapping away like everything was normal. Being a Catholic schoolboy, I felt uncomfortable and embarrassed and had to look away. The children were much braver. They'd stand and watch, hypnotized. *Perhaps remembering?*

It was a storybook evening. The children played, the infants wailed, and the adults took turns playing guitar and singing songs. I felt the situation was unique, something special, and I enjoyed every moment.

Dahlia told me her mom would be staying over for a couple of days and asked if she could use the room I was sleeping in.

"Sure . . . I sleep on the couch most of the time anyway. Actually, it works out perfect. You guys are in good shape with the ranch, and your mom will be here to help you, so I should head back to the city to see if I got that waiter's job. I can feed the animals in the morning and then head out . . . get an early start, beat the weekend traffic."

Everyone agreed it was a good plan and what we should do. They thanked me profusely, almost to the point of embarrassment. I was the one who was grateful. This was an experience that I would not soon forget. I told them I was going to write about it someday. Before turning in, I popped my head into the bedroom to say goodnight. The floor was covered with mattresses, and everyone was snuggled in, listening to bedtime stories. They invited me to stay and listen, but I declined, saying I was exhausted and needed a good night's sleep. The three of us laughed and said goodnight.

"What's so funny Mommy?" Jewel asked.

******

In the morning, the rooster crowed, and Serge had breakfast ready. Dahlia and the kids were still sleeping. He made peach pancakes with bacon and eggs, orange juice, toast, and coffee. I ate like a vacuum cleaner, not picking my head until I was done. My belly full, I took care of the barn business, said goodbye to Tom the barn cat, and went to the house to pack. When I was all set to go, Serge gave me a big long hug, thanking me again. Dahlia came out of the bedroom to say goodbye, hugging me, almost crying.

"Andy, you are wonderful, thank you!"

"Anytime, Dahlia. I'm the one who should thank you. I'll be in touch, Serge."

"I'll walk ya out, Andy."

I put my bags in the Karmen Ghia and started her up.

"Andy, on the way home, stop in North Beach at Alex Cowen's auto shop and get those gears fixed. I've already called, and it's all taken care of. He'll be expecting you. First stop, right?"

"Gotcha! . . . thanks Serge, I'll —"

"Don't start . . . Love ya, man."

The car was running and shifting fine. I got on the interstate in Grass Valley and had clear sailing all the way to San Francisco. *First stop . . . Alex Cowen's auto shop!*

Rainy Days

On rainy days I don't shave.
I drink beer, eat dark chocolates and write with great delight.
I only break to smoke a cigarette or feed the cat.
I'll water the Bonsai's and then work until eight
when it's time to cook myself a steak
and ruminate about what I've written.
The house is a mess,
but I'm happy about what I've accomplished.
All is well in the gentile shire.

ONE ACT PLAYS

Cliché's

A PLAY IN ONE ACT

Characters:

Arius: Tall, early forties, wearing a trench coat. A good-looking fellow with a con man's smile. He is a wanderer.

St. Cloud: Mid-height, balding, dressed in a poorly fitting black suit that is brought to life by a bright green tie. He is Arius's travel companion.

Albrecht: Dwarf like man with long hair and a beard. He is wearing baggy pants and a vest that barely covers his hairy body.

(Leaving a railroad tunnel stage left, Arius and St. Cloud enter following the track. Arius has a knapsack on his shoulder. St. Cloud carry's a blanket and water jug.)

Arius: I am hoping to achieve the enlightened state of ambivalence.

St. Cloud: Be careful what you wish for.

Arius: Bliss is when you don't give a crap about anything.

St. Cloud: Best thing since sliced bread.

Arius: Bet your bottom dollar. You're totally free to stop and think about something, . . . or, move on.

St. Cloud: (shaking his head in agreement) The best of all possible worlds.

Arius: Goes without saying. That's why I chose the life of a mendicant.

St. Cloud: You mean a hobo?

Arius: A voyeur onto life, . . . an explorer, an examiner; except for one's own life of course. Unattached, unencumbered, free to turn your back on the world and follow your heart.

St. Cloud: I watch myself like a frog watches a fly.

Arius: Free and easy.

St Cloud: Free as a bird?

Arius: Fresh as a daisy.

St. Cloud: If we're so free, how come we have to keep moving?

Arius: Rolling stones gather no moss.

St. Cloud: But suppose the road ends?

Arius: The suppose ta's never arrive and are usually lies. Who knows what tomorrow will bring? . . . Buddha was a mendicant. So was Jesus.

St. Cloud: You're not them.

Arius: And they'll never be me!

St. Cloud: I won't hold it against them.

Arius: I too (*pointing to the sky*) will do something great! Bigger than Socrates! More powerful than Charlie Chaplin or Dr. Phil!

St. Cloud: All I ever wanted was a dog and pony show.

Arius: And a dog and pony show you shall have. The finest! If P.T. Barnum could do it, so can you. . . . Just think small!

St. Cloud: Stop poking your finger in the sky's eye.

Arius: Oops (*looking up*), sorry, sky. You never said. How did you ever get a name like St. Cloud?

St. Cloud: I think it was the name of the lady who made out my birth certificate. I can't be sure.

Arius: What about your mother and father?

St. Cloud: They changed their name to fit mine, so . . . no problem.

Arius: Don't take any wooden nickels, my friend—

St. Cloud: No one's ever offered.

Arius: As it should be. . . . Ah! this looks like a good place to camp.

St. Cloud: Until a train comes by. I prefer the highway.

Arius: Not here, *(pointing)* in the clearing over there. Look . . . already we have a fire pit and a log for a pillow. Who could ask for more?

St. Cloud: Until a train comes . . . *(pacing)* then all hell breaks loose. *(he becomes excited as he speaks)* The earth trembles and convulses. The roar of the train grows to be demons escaping from the underworld. *(He puts up his hands to protect his head)* You pull your blanket over your head, hoping the apocalypse will pass. When it does, you try to get back to sleep, and just when your body relaxes, another train steamrolls through your nervous system, and you're a wreck again. By morning, you've developed spasms.

Arius: An existential nightmare. We'll make the best of an unpleasant situation.

St. Cloud: I'd rather have ear plugs.

Arius: Ah, . . . man's best friend. Pull up a chair; I'll fill the teakettle. St. Cloud, tonight we feast on an epicurean delight . . . pork and beans.

St. Cloud: A pig in a poke?

Arius: Beats a can of worms.

St. Cloud: Not without bread to soak up the gravy.

Arius: Man does not live by bread alone!

St. Cloud: It'd be nice to have a bit once in a while, that's all.

Arius: As luck would have it *(reaching into his trench coat pocket),* I was able to rescue a half loaf of Wonder Bread from a dumpster we passed back at the crossroads.

St. Cloud: The luck of the Irish! God bless the man who invented dumpsters. Garbage in—garbage out, feast, or famine.

Arius: Well said stout fellow; give and take, share and share alike and all that.

St. Cloud:(reaching into his pocket) And I will bring biscotti to the banquet.

Arius: I thought I saw you skulking around the picnic tables in the park when I used the bathroom there. (sternly) Did anyone see you?

St. Cloud: I don't believe so. They were all down by the lake. (*he starts a fire*) Carpe diem! . . . All's fair in love and war.

Arius: Ya' gotta' do wat ya' gotta' do. Cut and dried. (putting the beans into the pot and filling the kettle with water) It's Darwinian! The survival of the misfits.

St. Cloud: They didn't miss it. Otherwise I would have had a knuckle sandwich by now.

Arius: Yet another reason to keep moving.

St. Cloud: It's the law of the jungle . . . while the cats away the—

Arius: Yes, yes, the wisdom of the ages. I say, . . . is that Albrecht coming from the tunnel?

St. Cloud: Yes, and he appears to have tied one on; he's tighter than a drum.

Arius: Three sheets to the wind. . . . Sit perfectly still. Maybe he won't notice us.

St. Cloud: (*wrapping themselves in the blanket*) Like two peas in a pod.

Arius: (*in a loud whisper*) He sees the fire. He's coming this way.

St. Cloud: He's looking for his ring. He said they forged it in fire.

Arius: He doesn't see us, or the food . . . I hope he doesn't knock everything over.

St. Cloud: He's poking the fire, looking for the ring.

Arius: Listen!!! He's grumbling something.

(from underneath the blanket, they both lean forward to listen)

Albrecht: Where are you? *(wiping tears from his eyes, he returns to the tracks and continues his trek)*

Arius: (with a sigh) He looks like a world-weary cave dweller, walking through the shadows of time.

St. Cloud: He said his relatives were all dwarfs.

Arius: That's pretty old.

St. Cloud: Maybe even older!

Arius: Better late than never —

St. Cloud: Only time will tell.

Arius: And time is of the essence!

St. Cloud: Bah, it's the spitting image of yesterday. . . . Let's eat already!

Arius: Now we're cooking. Seize the day, as you say. Sit . . . I am happy to serve *(reaching into the other pocket of his trench coat)*, and from the very same dumpster, I have procured Earl Grey's Deluxe for our evening tea.

St. Cloud: Who has it better than us!

Arius: Ah! *(hand to his ear)* my Muse beckons. We have some things we wanna' run by ya.'

St. Cloud: That can't be good. The less said, the better. For all intents and purposes, explaining things is a last-ditch effort to —

Arius: Please allow me my moment in the sun, or in this case, the fire. My hour upon the stage, my fifteen minutes of fame. Hear my bid for glory!

St. Cloud: Okay. Just don't talk fast while I eat. I get confused.

Arius: Words and ideas are like rivers and streams. They all flow from dreams (stirring the pot) and the beans. Food for the soul.

St. Cloud: Now you're a poet?

Arius: With imagination! We create the world.

St. Cloud: With imagination, you describe the world. It has nothing to do with what's really there.

Arius: A trifling detail. We are on to better things. Call the hounds and join the hunt for new ideas.

St. Cloud: You're running in circles

Arius: Of course I am. I'm looking to square things, ya' know. It's the only way —

St. Cloud: Beware! The road to hell is paved with good

intentions.

Arius: And so is the road to heaven, so how ya' gonna' know which is which?

St. Cloud: Oh well, that's a topic best discussed after dessert and a couple of brandies. All's well that ends well. . . . How are you gonna' get people to listen to these new ideas?

Arius: I will simply point out to them that I don't make mistakes and that they should put their trust in my record and my accomplishments.

St. Cloud: You don't do nothin'; how can you make mistakes? What accomplishments? It's all talk, no action.

Arius: What! (pacing) So now you're gonna start breaking cookies?

St. Cloud: If I have to. It's a dirty job, but somebody's got to do it. What mistakes haven't you made? (*Arius pokes the fire as he talks*)

Arius: Well, . . . we have been in Florida for six months, and there hasn't been an earthquake. Not a single avalanche. Just as I predicted.

St. Cloud: And the wind-up is?

Arius: When the world is troubled, you gotta' learn to dance.

St. Cloud: Now you sound like Lawrence Welk.

Arius: A hero amongst heroes. . . . Trip the lights fantastic!

St Cloud: A Fandango might be appropriate. I believe I have a pair of castanets in my bag.

Arius: You never cease to amaze me. I could have sworn you were a 'pas de deux' man.

St Cloud: Still water runs deep.

(They both dance around the fire. St. Cloud playing the castanets and Arius using the blanket as a cape, twirling it in the air)

Arius: Where did ya' learn that fancy footwork?

St Cloud: In a cantina in Tijuana. How 'bout you?

Arius: I took some LSD at a rock concert outside Toledo. It made such an impression on me my muscle memory kicks in whenever I hear music. I become a slave to Terpsichore. I live to serve the muse.

St. Cloud: Not unexpected!

Arius: Let it be known (emphatically pointing to the sky while dancing) ... I am a thespian . . . and there are things that only thespians can say. I subscribe to that privilege and shall avail myself of it. I shall darn the Phrygian Cap.

St. Cloud: Like the court jester.

Arius: ACH! How many nights have I wept with Rigoletto? (sic)

St. Cloud: It's the price we pay for our rebellious natures.

(*out of breath, Arius sits on the log and stokes the fire*)

Arius: I've got to do something. My life as a lounge lizard didn't pan out. It came to nothing.

St. Cloud: (sitting next to Arius, arm around his shoulder) Loud music is rarely harmonious Arius. You're better off being a mendicant.

Arius: (Jumping up) Truer words have never been spoken. I will continue as a savant and try to save the world from itself. The blind leading the blind through blood, sweat, and tears.

St. Cloud: I, for one, am willing to invest everything I own in your new idea.

Arius: Thank you, St. Cloud, that means a lot to me.

St. Cloud: So, when we gonna' start? (rubbing his hands together)

Arius: Well, I have to make plans and all —

St. Cloud: That's what you said last year!

Arius: (warming his hands over the fire) Good planning, good execution, make for good results!

St. Cloud: It's déjà vu all over again. Same old, same old. Before we go any further, what's this new idea about?

Arius: It's all about the power of clichés. I want to help people to understand that all they need to know is ensconced in the clichés they use every day. And they are great mnemonic devices as well. You take a bunch of facts, wrap them in a cliché like a burrito, . . . and you have it all in a nutshell.

St. Cloud: Imagine that . . . clichés and burritos, who'd a eva thunk. When do we get started?

Arius: You've already asked that question. You're only allowed to ask a question once. Got it?

St. Cloud: I believe so. When will you begin being a wise mendicant?

Arius: I'm gonna sleep on it tonight. John the squirrel told me there are opportunities in Cincinnati for lounge lizards, and somehow or other, I have developed an urge for alligator boots.

St. Cloud: They do make everything electric.

Arius: Yes, but Cincinnati, this time of year, I don't know?

St. Cloud: Any time of year! Last time we were in Cincinnati, I spent the night in jail.

Arius: A case of mistaken identity.

St. Cloud; You told the police I was you!

Arius: I got you out, come morning!

St. Cloud: By promising to leave town before sunrise. We may not be welcome there, I think.

Arius: Things to consider. I'll sleep on it.

St. Cloud: You do, do that well.

Arius: Thank you, St. Cloud. Now, are you going to give me a part of the blanket?

St. Cloud: (grudgingly) When you gonna' get your own blanket?

Arius: When yours falls apart.

St. Cloud: Just as I had suspected! All you have ever wanted was half of my blanket.

Arius: I will always refuse the whole of it. It wouldn't be same without you.

St. Cloud: Whatever! *(he leans his head on the log, pulling the blanket to his chin in a fetal position)* It's your turn for fire watch tonight.

Arius: As you wish. Goodnight, St. Cloud. *(he stretches out, rests his head on the log, covers himself with the blanket, which only reaches his knees.)* This pillow smells like farts.

St. Cloud: You were sitting on it while you were talking. Just your run-of-the-mill brain farts. Go to sleep, Arius.

(The train will pass three times during the night. Stage time, one minute between. During the quiet intervals, Arius will awake and tend to the fire. He sleeps through the roar of the train passing as St. Cloud has spasms underneath the blanket. After the third train, with the sun rising backstage, Arius prepares the morning tea. He takes two stale biscuits from his pocket and places them on a grate on top of the kettle to heat them. St. Cloud pokes his head out from under his covering to see if the coast is clear and it is safe to reenter the world. He checks several times, recoils into a tight ball, and springs from under his blanket)

St. Cloud: I am ready to begin the day.

(St. Cloud circles the fire, trying to appease his cramped muscles. He stops at the cardinal points of the compass to shake off a spasm or two, then continues around the hearth. Arius tends to the fire and kettle.)

Arius: What's that you're doing? You're making me dizzy!

St. Cloud: I'm walking off my spasms.

Arius: Well, walk somewhere else. It makes my head spin. You don't me want to fall into the fire . . . or do you?

St. Cloud: Of course, not . . . (he gives each leg a good shake)

Two minutes I've been awake, and already you're complaining.

Arius: You're right, St. Cloud, I'm sorry . . . it's my Anhedonia[8] flaring up again. I will think of more pleasant things and ease the stress. Here, come, sit and have a biscuit. It will more than make up for my rudeness.

(*St. Cloud has periodic spasms as they sit on the log with their tea and biscuits*)

St. Cloud: Pleasure is stress too, ya know. (mouth full)

Arius: Yes . . . and the Amygdala demands both. As it was written, so it shall be—

(*Arius pauses, deep in thought. St. Cloud, waiting for Arius to finish what he was saying, gets up and gives each of his legs a shake and sits down again*)

St. Cloud: Stop screaming.

Arius: I didn't say a word—

St. Cloud: The silence is deafening.

Arius: I'll try to keep it down.

St. Cloud: Please do; you'll wake the neighbors. So, what's it gonna' be? What has sleep decided for us today? . . . because I'm not going to Cincinnati—

---

[8] The inability to feel pleasure.

Arius: Neither am I. I think I'll continue with my plan for changing the world.

St. Cloud: So you're not satisfied with the sun, the moon, the stars. The flowers, the Ocean, the—

Arius: No, no, no, they're okay. It's the percepts I'm after. Change the percepts — you change the thinking. A faulty 'a priori' creates false dichotomies, which create twisted percepts and causes humanity to walk with a limp. We will begin there and rid ourselves of our braces.

St. Cloud: (approvingly) That sounds Phrygian, very Phrygian.

Arius: I got it from a guy who lived in a wine jar in Athens.[9] He was a mendicant too.

St. Cloud: I'm impressed. . . . But people seem to like these 'a priori'.

Arius: There ya' go again. Must you always be negative? . . . It never ends. To those people, I would say, to each his own, because water seeks its own level and there ain't no changing that.

St. Cloud: Then why do we have to do anything at all?

---

[9] Diogenes the Cynic

Arius: Point taken . . . but a journey of a thousand miles begins with a single step, so, *(Gesturing)* we must be on our way.

St. Cloud: What's your hurry? You're always in a hurry.

Arius: There's a lot to do.

St. Cloud: There's always a lot to do. But we don't do anything!

Arius: It takes just as long to do nothing as it takes to do something, and it is often the more difficult. *(Arius packs the pot and kettle into his knapsack. St. Cloud folds his blanket and throws it over his shoulder, water jug in hand. They enter the tracks.)* Now, where was I?

St. Cloud: Clichés and burritos.

Arius: Yes! And what to do with them.

St. Cloud: Ideas have always been marketable.

Arius: And we're on the silk road. (stopping in front of the tunnel) I will be a guiding light.

St. Cloud: Well shine a little light this way will ya'! . . .We should go, NOTHING is waiting for us. *(they disappear into the tunnel and continue talking, now with an echo)*

Arius: Yes, of course. As I was saying, a good cliché is worth a thousand words!

St. Cloud: I avoid them like the plague.

Curtain Falls

Metamorphosis
A PLAY IN ONE ACT

Characters:

Charlene: Statuesque woman, mid-thirties, blond shoulder-length hair. A champion of all causes.

Edward: A successful New York lawyer. Tall, good-looking with an athletic build. Shallow and full of hubris.

Celeste: The cook. She has been with the couple for years.

Dad: Charles Dobbs, successful businessman, gruff in manner, and known as a straight talker.

Mom: Arlene Dobbs, socialite belonging to many of the leading social organizations.

(All internal dialogue is heard through speakers.)

SCENE ONE

The curtain rises to Charlene cooking breakfast in the kitchen of a high-rise apartment. The picture windows behind her frame a view of central park and the New York skyline. Next to the kitchen, before the windows, is the dining room table. The apartment has an open floor plan, with a step down into the living room. The bedrooms are stage left and right. It is early morning as Edward comes out of the bedroom on the right. He opens the front door, picks up his newspaper, and tosses it on the table. Putting his arm around Charlene's waist, he bends over the stove to examine the food.

Edward: All of my favorites. Pancakes, eggs over easy, bacon, and coffee. I've never had it so good.

Charlene: Hold that thought. Go sit down; it's almost ready. [I don't know what's come over me.]

(Edward sits at the table, opens the newspaper, and scans the headlines)

Edward: I'm getting a little suspicious. Last night a gourmet dinner, then Olympic sex, and now my favorite breakfast. You haven't cooked this in years. We haven't had sex like that in ages.

Charlene: Remember that! [*I was shameless last night*]

Edward: (*arranging his newspaper*) I'm expecting that you've come up with a fantastic new scheme, and you want to soften me up. Which you have rather well, I might say. So whenever you're ready. (*Charlene brings his breakfast to the table*)

Charlene: Bon appetite, darling. (*she returns with her own plate of cantaloupe, raspberries, and oblong tea. She sits across from him, watching him eat voraciously*)

Edward: [*She's still crazy about me.*] This is wonderful, Charlene!

Charlene: I don't know how you function after shoveling all that into your system.

Edward: A wise man once said, "You can take the boy out of the country, but you can't take West Virginia out of the man." Or something like that.

Charlene: (*spooning off slices of cantaloupe as she speaks*) And who was that?

Edward: My father. I think?

Charlene: Edward, I have something very important to tell you. I am going to have an operation. It has already been scheduled, and we begin the process next week.

Edward: My God, Charlene, what is it? Why have you waited until now to tell me? What do you have? What is the prognosis? (*he gets up and begins pacing*) Are you going to die?

Charlene: No, no, nothing like that. It's not life-threatening or anything. More at elective surgery.

Edward: You mean all of this attention you've been showing me is because you're going to have a facelift?

Charlene: No, no, it's a lot more than a facelift. Edward, please sit down. (*taking a deep breath*) Edward, I am going to have gender reassignment surgery. Husband of mine . . . I'm going to have a sex-change operation. (*Edward sits, looks at her dumbfounded as he struggles to process the news*) Isn't it wonderful? I've already started the hormone therapy, and the doctors tell me it's going along fine. Soon you'll be seeing me in an entirely different way. Edward, say something*! [My God . . . it's the hormone therapy that's making me act this way]*

Edward: (*Getting up, he paces again.*) I know! . . . this is a movie plot for one of those groups you volunteer for. You're testing it out on me . . . to see how it goes.

Charlene: (*she takes the dishes to the sink, stands behind the island*) No, it's for real. But as a matter of fact, there are negotiations for the rights to my story taking place as we speak. A book deal with movie rights! We're working out the details.

Edward: And who are we?

Charlene: Gina and me. She's been taking care of the business part.

Edward: Your friend from Facebook?

Charlene: Yup, she's brilliant. She also has interviews set up with Rachel Madcow and Keith Uberwuss. Her negotiating made them double their offer. She's been wonderful! And very supportive over the past two years. She's been helping me make the tough decisions.

Edward: So, . . . someone from social media is your primary consultant. And even though your husband is one of the best attorneys in the city, your Facebook friend is handling your legal. . . . Didn't you tell me your friend Gina was a real-estate person?

Charlene: Yup. She reads people like a book. You should have seen her with those publishers. (*taking a deep breath*) All of this hasn't been easy for me, Edward. Especially in the beginning, and Gina has stayed with me each step of the way.

Edward: Remind me to thank her later . . . (*sitting with head in hands*) You sound quite taken with her.

Charlene: I do love her, but not in the way you're thinking. (*walking to the window, staring at the city below*) Edward, I am a man cruelly imprisoned inside a woman's body. I am black, homosexual, with a voracious appetite for young athletes. It started about two years ago and is slowly becoming my new reality. I feel like I'm wearing a diver's wet suit with a broken zipper, and I can't get out of it.

Edward: Two years ago, . . . I remember! That's when you were working on that documentary about the Bay Area LGBT community. Man was I glad when that was over . . . you were bitchy for months.

Charlene: Bitchy is no longer appropriate in my case, Edward. Think . . . (*dropping her voice*) 'You were a hard-on for months, buddy'. Verbiage is indicative of thought process, and we must be mindful of whom we are addressing so that we choose the correct pronouns and gender signals.

Edward: Sounds complicated.

Charlene: Perhaps, but necessary. You might hurt someone's feelings and make them feel uncomfortable. You don't want to do that. (*matter- of- factly*)

Edward: I don't? . . . Are you suggesting I tread on pins and needles because someone might be a basket case? How will I know what to say? (*sarcastically*) Is there a manual or something?

Charlene: It's coming out soon . . . a complete guide on how to treat LGBT people. How to speak with love and respect so the world can be a better place. Only the most hateful people would deny basic human rights.

Edward: This PC crap has gone too far . . . you people are making fools of yourselves. You want to reduce people to stuttering paranoids, afraid of almost everything. A nation of mental patients.

Charlene: They said you would respond like this.

Edward: Who are they?

Charlene: Facebook, of course! and Twitter and all the others too.

Edward: Of course! . . . second party, third party, verification by the numbers. Please, Charlene, sit, let's talk this out. (*trying to get organized*) I should write this down. I need a pen and paper.

Charlene: (*sitting across from him*) In the top desk draw.

Edward: (*returning to the table*) Okay . . . Let's get started. Help me get this straight. You are a person who is a black male homosexual, imprisoned in a white female's body, and are hopelessly attracted to athletes.

Charlene: That's a good start.

Edward: And you wish to transition, using sex re-assignment surgery, to correct this mis-assignment of gender made by mother nature.

Charlene: That's right. Are we talking here? . . . because you're making this sound like a deposition?

Edward: Sorry, it's my default response, it's the way I sort things out. . . . I'm a little confused. Wouldn't you be in a better position to bed your athletes as a woman?

Charlene: (she goes to the sink to wash the dishes) You'd be surprised!

Edward: Maybe I would.

Charlene: Besides, I like to do the penetrating.

Edward: Well, you don't need surgery for that! There are devices—

Charlene: Edward, please! . . . it's not the same thing. In my heart and soul, I am a man who is attracted to other men. It would be a travesty to strap something on, only to have to take it off. I want to have sex the natural way. I have my needs.

Edward: Sooo . . . gender assignment therapy is the natural way?

Charlene: Its science assisting nature.

Edward: Oh, I see. (walks to the window, stares at the park below, thinking)

[*This might be a blessing in disguise. This could work in my favor. Who would blame me for wanting out of this marriage? The woman is nuts! She has championed every wackjob 'cause celebre' she could find for years. It's a regular topic of conversation with our friends.*] (returning to the table) . . . Charlene, do you remember a couple of years back when you wanted to sell everything and move to the Amazon to live in a treehouse.

Charlene: Yes, we were trying to save the rainforest. That fell thru though, when the founder of the movement was caught using the foundation's funds as his own back account.

Edward: And if it were not for a delay in the wire transfer, you'd be one poor man, trapped in a woman's body. Where would the money for all the procedures come from? I don't think your parents are going to pay for this one.

Charlene: They don't have to. The book and movie deal will pay for most of the cost, and Gina has set up a 'go fund me page,' which should take care of the rest.

Edward: Ah yes, Gina! [*thank you, Gina*] . . . I'm just suggesting it might be wise to move slowly on this one. Not so easy to reverse this stuff [*The more you question this, the stronger her resolve will become*] . . . Just curious, how are people going to know that you're a black person? I mean, you're all white, Charlene. If the term 'Karen' applied to anyone, it would be you.

Charlene: I have people to help me with that too. The community has set me up with a black history professor at NYU to help me purge myself of the privilege and the bias of the white supremacist culture I was mistakenly born into. Also, a friend on Facebook knows someone in Harlem who can supply me with Melanin to help darken my skin to its natural color. He says that after a few treatments and visits to the tanning salon, I will be dark as the night.

Edward: [*I wonder who will pay for the room?*]

Charlene: Everyone is saying that this is the way of the future, and I will be at the forefront of an emerging technology.

Edward: Charlene, we have to think about this. It sounds like you're putting yourself at considerable risk, and it might prove dangerous.

Charlene: (sitting) I am a part of what will be a genuine change in the coming new world.

Edward: Where Mad Max reigns! It's all been done before you know. It's been called the dark ages, amongst other things. I don't think it would have helped to hug a Visigoth.

Charlene: It will be different this time. We've learned from our mistakes. All goods and services will be available to all people on demand, which will eliminate the need for pillaging or hoarding.

Edward: None of this sounds very realistic. You can't just hope things will work out. We need to think this thru. We'll skip the cancel culture debate for now. Let's clean our own house first. Do your parents know about these life changes you're going to make?

Charlene: No, I was hoping to have you by my side when I told them.

Edward: They're going to' blame me, you know. They're gonna' say that I didn't satisfy you, that I made you gay. I can hear it now, your mom's shrill voice "If you bedded her properly, she wouldn't be doing this."

Charlene: I'll explain it to them. They know I have my needs, and they will listen. This has nothing to do with you, Edward. You've been a good husband and have made a good life for us.   You're as good in the sack as anyone I've known, and you know that.

Edward: (*smiling*) Well, I know that and you know that but what about everyone else? (*Smiling again*) Or have you been boasting again about what a good ride you get?

Charlene: [*Good Lord!*] Like I said, Edward, this has nothing to do with our marriage. It has to do with how I feel. It has to do with being true to my nature. I had planned on calling our friends to give them a heads up on the exciting changes taking place. Since you feel so strongly about this, I will be sure to emphasize your prowess in the sac.

Edward: (pacing again) [*capitalize on your loss*] How will this affect my practice? What will my colleagues say? Charlene, have you considered how this would affect me? . . . Obliviously not. We can't stay together after this gets out. I'm not living with a gay guy.

Charlene: Edward, I have my needs.

Edward: But what about me? How will I go on? This has turned my entire world upside down.

Charlene: We thought you could just continue with your life if you kept the practice and the apartment.

Edward: (turns away, mimes a fist pump) *[Yes!]*

Charlene: Hell, you're all set up for a bachelors' dream life. I know this is inconvenient for you, Edward, but we think it's for the best.

Edward: We again! Must you humiliate me?

Charlene: I'm sorry Edward, It's all for the best--

Edward: You keep saying that! Maybe the best for you. What about me? I'm the one who is losing everything. But . . . if we can both agree to a mutually acceptable arrangement, it should lessen the pain and should all go rather quickly, without a hitch.

Charlene: That's what we're hoping for.

Edward: So, pretty much, we both pick up our toys and go home.

Charlene: I'm hoping to keep the house in Woodstock. I will need a quiet place to live while I make the transition.

Edward: That makes sense . . . what about the cars?

Charlene: I'll keep the Land Rover. I want nothing to do with the Jaguar.

Edward: I'm kind of attached to the Land Rover. Wouldn't a pickup truck better suit the new you? *[The apartment and the Jag! You're on a roll, don't blow it]*

Charlene: Let's not get greedy, Edward. But I do insist that I keep the Grandfather Clock. It has been such a comfort to me over the years and has such broad shoulders.

Edward: If you must. Let's get this down on paper.

Charlene: I've always admired the solid and sure way you do things, Edward. That's what attracted me to you when we first met.

Edward: And you were wild and free and so refreshing. But that was twelve years ago, and now is now. Let's stay focused on what we're doing. Let's see, (writing) Article 1 . . . Real property. Edward Hictor to receive the Manhattan apartment and its furnishings . . . except the grandfather clock. Charlene

Dobbs to receive the country house in Woodstock, New York.

Charlene: And all its contents!

Edward: And all its contents. E. Hictor to receive the Jaguar and C. Dobbs to receive the Land Rover. (looking winsome) I'm going to miss the country house.

Charlene: Find yourself a place over in Callicoon. You've always loved fishing the Delaware. I'll tell you what Edward, you get a place in Callicoon, and I'll throw in the fishing gear . . . and the gun safe. If I want fish to eat, I'll go to the store. And I'm sure I will not be killing any animals just so I can eat. (taking his hand) I just want you to be happy.

Edward: That's very decent of you, Charlene. Thank you. Okay, let's stay focused here.

Charlene: I must say you're taking this much better than I expected.

Edward: It is what it is, Charlene. We have to move on. The world's not going to stop because you want to have a sex change. We have to make the best of it.

Charlene: I thought you would be at least a *little* sad. Gina said you might need a day or two to mourn. You're *supposed* to mourn Edward!

Edward: Well, the "WE" is wrong and the "Supposed to Be's" are never what they're supposed to be.

Charlene: I thought you'd mourn at least a little.

Edward: I mourned while you were doing the dishes. You know, before you make any announcements, I think you should tell your parents. It would be a killer if they heard about this somewhere else.

Charlene: I'm going to call them and invite them for dinner tonight. I'll tell them then.

Edward: Best to get that over with and out of the way.

Charlene: I appreciate your help, Edward.

Edward: My pleasure. Now, back to work. (the curtain comes down slowly as they discuss the division of property) Bank accounts, TDA's, IRA's, etc. will revert to the original owners, prior to the marriage . . .

Curtain Falls

SCENE TWO

The curtain rises to the same set. The dinner table has been set, and a cook is at the stove preparing the evening meal. Charlene enters stage left in her bathrobe and speaks to the cook. Edward enters stage right.

Edward: Charlene, did the maid pick up the dry cleaning? I can't find any clean shirts.

Charlene: She's moved all my stuff into the guest bedroom, so we have rearranged everything. Shirts are on the top shelf of the chifforobe.

(They both return to their rooms. The cook is finishing the dinner preparations. The intercom buzzer sounds, and Charlene pokes her head out of the door.)

Charlene: Edward, can you get that, please?

Edward: Okay! *(rushing out, fixing his tie)* Hello . . . yes, you can send them right up Sydney, thank you. *(yelling to Charlene)* It's your parents. They're on their way up. *(disappearing into his room, Charlene runs out and up to the cook.)*

Charlene: Celeste, would you zip me up, please?

Celeste: Of course. Mrs. Dobb's Everything is in the oven and should stay warm for an hour or so. (Charlene turns around) And you look fabulous in that black dress, Mrs. Dobbs. Or should I say, Mr. Dobbs! *(laughing, taking her coat and bag from the closet, she winks as she exits. Charlene is on the way back to her room when the door chime sounds)*

Charlene: Edward, can you get that? I have to put on my face. (she disappears into her room as Edward comes out, slipping on his suit jacket, to answer the door)

Edward: Greetings! Welcome, come on in. Let me take your things. We sent the help home early so it would be just family tonight. Ah, Champagne! Let me put this on ice. Come, make yourselves comfortable. Dinner is all set. Ready when we are. Can I get you anything?

Dad: I'll have a scotch and soda.

Mom: And I'll have a white wine. *(Edward mixes the drinks)* All we talked about on the way here was the 'Big News' Charlene has for us. She said it would be a big surprise.

Edward: *(handing them their drinks)* Oh, it's a big surprise all right. (returns to the bar to get his own)

Dad: Any chance we could get a preview?

Mom: Should I open a registry at Bergdorf's?

Edward: *(smiling)* I better not say anything. Charlene would be furious if I ruined her surprise.

(Charlene enters)

<u>*Charlene:*</u> Mommy-Daddy, so good to see you. (hugging them) Thank you so much for coming on such short notice.

<u>*Dad:*</u> It was short notice—

<u>*Mom:*</u> Charlene, you look absolutely beautiful in that dress.

Charlene: Why, thank you, Momma. Sit, please.

Edward: Would you like something to drink, Charlene?

Charlene: Whisky and soda (lowering her voice) make it a double!

<u>*Edward:*</u> Charlene!

Charlene: *(to her parents)* Something I saw in a movie.

<u>*Mom:*</u> We're excited to hear about your 'Big News.' It's all we've talked about since you called.

Charlene: Well, it is big news, but it may not be what you're expecting.

<u>*Mom:*</u> Expecting . . . that's what I want to hear! Expecting.

<u>*Edward:*</u> Perhaps I should get us all another drink.

<u>**Charlene:**</u> Daddy, do you remember when I was a kid you told me that if I wanted to remove a band-aid, I should do it

quickly, in one fell swoop. You said to get it over with, rather than having the little bits of pain that come with doing it slow.

Daddy: Of course I do.

Charlene: Well, that's what I'm going to do. I'm just gonna come right out with it. Mom-Dad, I have been living a lie for several years now. I have tried to put it aside—

Edward: Here we go—

Charlene: I have tried to put it aside and deny my true nature but to no avail. It has caused Edward and myself a great deal of pain—

Edward: I didn't even know about it until this morning.

Charlene: Mom, Dad, I want you to know I am a man trapped in a woman's body, and I'm going to have treatments and surgery to correct nature's mistake.

(Dad gulps his drink, Mom drops her wineglass in her lap. Edward rushes over with a bar towel.)

Mom: There was no mistake, believe me . . . I was there!

Dad: I'll have that drink now, Edward.

Mom: Another wine here, please, and Edward . . . leave the bottle.

Edward: But wait, there's more.

Charlene: (squinting her eyes at him) Thank you, Edward. (turning to her parents) In my heart and soul and every fiber of my being, I am a black man, a homosexual man who is a prisoner inside a white woman's body.

Dad: Your kidding, right? This is just another one of your crazy schemes.

Mom: You'd never know by looking at you. (Mom is looking dazed and stares off while she speaks)

Charlene: Well, I've just started hormone therapy and will begin the surgical procedures after that.

Dad: You're not kidding, are you? You're serious.

Mom: I thought you were going to give us good news . . . like we're going to be grandparents.

Charlene: Mother . . . I'm thirty-seven years old. It would be kind of risky having a baby at my age.

Dad: And having a sex change operation at your age is not risky?

Mom: We were thinking you might even want to adopt.

Charlene: If you're so into adoption mother, why don't you adopt?

Mom: Because then we wouldn't be grandparents.

Dad: Not this time, Charlene. I will not pay for changing God's plan for creation. And I sure as hell know Edward won't be paying for it either. (fixing his eyes on Edward)

Mom: I'm with your father on this one.

Charlene: I don't need your help, Daddy. We have the financing all worked out.

Dad: (scowling at Edward) For someone who just learned about this morning, you sure have gotten a lot done.

Edward: Don't look at me. She's talking about Gina.

Dad: Who the hell is Gina?

Mom: She's from Facebook Charles. . . . Are you going to be Gina's husband, Charlene?

Charlene: And I have the whole LGBT community behind me for support.

Dad: I don't want to hear anything about no LBGGXYZ or whatever they're called today.

Charlene: Daddy, you sound bigoted and hostile.

Dad: Bullshit! I don't give a rat's ass who plays with whose pee-pee. I don't want to know their business. It's kind of creepy, the way you people are into everybody's personal life. A kind of voyeuristic perversion, if you ask me, keep it to yourselves.

Charlene: That sure sounds like hate speech to me. And no momma, I will not be Gina's husband . . . I told you I'm a homosexual man . . . not a lesbian

Mom: All of this business so you can have sex with a man? Isn't that what you have now? Edward is your husband.

Edward: She wants to do the penetrating.

Dad: You seem to be enjoying this, Edward.

Edward: No, Charles, it's just the way I handle things.

Charlene: I thought that too Daddy. And he hasn't mourned properly either.

Dad: (to Charlene) And you, *my son*, I do have a beef with your people. LEAVE THE SCHOOL CHILDREN ALONE! Let them be kids and live like kids. They have plenty of time to decide whose stinky parts they want to sniff. Let them ride their bikes, climb trees, go camping, and trick-or-treating.

Charlene: Daddy, you don't realize how hard it is for these abandoned children.

Dad: Neither do they until you tell them. (turning to Edward) Actually, there might be a way to make some money with all this foolishness. I can have one of my construction companies specialize in transgender bathrooms. If the government wants to accommodate these confused kids, then I say let's make something of it. With three bathrooms on every floor, it's a gold mine. We can specialize in schools. If we become the premier transgender bathroom company in the country, we'll have a jump on all the competition.

Edward: That's something I might be interested in. I'd like to get in on that.

Dad: I'll get back to you.

Mom: (to Charlene) Do you know which bathroom to use? Edward, how could you let this happen?

Edward: Believe me, it was the last thing on my mind.

Mom: If you had bedded her properly, this never would have happened.

Edward: (looking at Charlene) I told you so.

Mom: You were such a pretty little girl; everybody said so. Now you're going to have a mustache.

Charlene: What do you say we take a break and have the wonderful dinner Celeste made for us. It's all ready; I just have to serve it.

Dad: Who could eat at a time like this?

Mom: I might throw up.

Edward: Maybe just the hors d'oeuvres Charlene. (she leaves to prepare a tray. Speaking to her parents) You know, Charlene must be feeling like we're all ganging up on her about now.

Dad: We should have done it years ago. This girl has needed an intervention all her life. I blame you for this, Arlene, telling her she's special all those years, giving her rewards for accomplishing nothing.

Mom: Oh my! . . . What are the ladies at the Daughters of the American Revolution going to say?

Dad: I'm sure they will be very sympathetic.

Mom: Oh . . . yes, (having an epiphany) and they will all be very supportive. Esther Fox has a granddaughter who dresses like a Goth person, and Susan Elliot has not left her side since.

Edward: Do I detect a bit of Munchausen's?

Charlene: Now is not the time, Edward (placing the tray of hors d'oeuvres on the cocktail table).

Come, everyone, eat. You have to put something in your stomach other than alcohol.

Edward: You're right, Charlene. (helping himself to the food)

Charlene: (pacing while eating) I was hoping my family would be there for me. We feel your support is a necessary part of our success. They say If you really love me, you will support a world where everyone is free to be whomever they want to be.

Edward: (to Dad) The "We" she refers to are the actual participants of their little cabal. The "They say" is the collective wisdom of social media.

Dad: Thank you, Edward. Actually, that's quite useful.

(The curtain comes down slowly as the lights begin to fade. Mom is thoroughly inebriated.)

Mom: What should I call you? How will I introduce you to people?

Charlene: We were thinking about Charlie. It's close to Charlene and —

Mom: (gulping her wine) The little man in the boat is certainly in charge of that ship! Nothing I can do. It is what it is!

Curtain Falls

SCENE THREE
Six months later

(The curtain rises to Edward putting a coffee cartridge into the coffee maker. The set is the same minus the grandfather clock. He is rummaging thru the cabinets)

Edward: Where did she put my coffee mug? The damn maid has re-arranged everything. (*Finding it, he pours his coffee and takes a pastry to the end of the table. While staring out of the window, eating and drinking his coffee, the landline rings. Putting down the pastry, he picks up the receiver and answers.*) Hello? Yes . . . Cynthia! Hello, how are you? . . . I'm good, better than ever; busy as hell. . . . Cynthia, I'm gonna put you on speakerphone, my hands are kind of full, hold on. Hello? Are you there?

Cynthia: I'm here, Edward. I'm glad I caught you at home. I have a new phone. Lost everyone's numbers and have been calling around to bring it up to date.

Edward: It's good to hear from you, it's been a while! How are you and Ignazio doing? Still with the ballet? (continuing to eat and drink coffee while he listens)

Cynthia: We've been traveling a lot. Rome is home right now. We had a huge imbroglio last month, and Ignazio is in Barcelona, staying with friends until things calm down. It is so annoying being around temperamental artists all the time, Edward. I know people think it a romantic lifestyle, living and traveling with a world-famous dancer, but it gets old. I'm afraid the bloom of this romance has faded along with the flowers on the Spanish Steps. I'll be moving back to the States.

Edward: I'm sorry to hear that. You both seemed so happy last time I saw you. Marriage is hard when everyone wants a piece of you. They leave no time for family —

Cynthia: Oh well, time to move on. I'll be setting up in New York. Opening a lingerie line. I found a shop on Madison Avenue that will be just perfect. . . . How are things there?

Edward: Well, the leaves are changing in Central Park. It's like a carpet. The sky is as gray as the buildings —

Cynthia: I'm not asking about the weather. I've been hearing some pretty strange things about Charlene wanting to become a man? What's going on? I can't believe what people are saying. Are we all talking about the same Charlene?

Edward: Probably most of what your hearing is true. She's out-done herself this time. She claimed she was a gay African American man with an insatiable appetite for athletes. She said her homo homunculus was bigger than she was and could no longer live with a lie. Turns out she's a Buddha-shaped black guy with a yellow cap and red sneakers.

Cynthia: Wouldn't she have a better chance bagging her athletes as a beautiful, rich, white lady?

Edward: I asked her the same thing. She said I'd be surprised. . . . She had it all set up with a friend of hers. Expenses, surgery, treatments all paid for by 'go fund me' and a documentary or movie deal about her transition.

Cynthia: Really . . . I'm impressed.

Edward: But the craziness didn't stop there. They screwed up her hormone meds, and everything went haywire. She became a nympho instead of a homo.

Cynthia: Nothings simple anymore.

Edward: Luckily, I was able to put a rush on our divorce because of the medical contingencies. We just slipped by before she changed her mind. She would have contested, and you know how the courts are here. A woman is always the victim, even when she's the perpetrator.

Cynthia: I hope the Italian courts feel the same way.

Edward: By the time 'Her people' realized they were giving her the wrong meds, it was too late. She was loving them, refused to give them up. Now she's a sports groupie, following college basketball teams around the country. Her partner is suing her for breach of contract, her parents won't speak to her, and the 'go fund me' people want their money back. But she doesn't care.

Cynthia: How are her parents handling all this?

Edward: They were livid at first. Arlene was inebriated for days. But then they turned it around. Charles made one of his construction companies specialize in the needs of transgender people. He submitted a proposal to some of his friends on the city council, and now it's called 'The New York Plan for Transgender Accommodations.' He has preliminary contracts with L.A., San Francisco, Seattle, and Portland. He tells me they are branching out to Chicago, Madison, and

Minneapolis. So far, I have a two-hundred percent return on my investment.

Cynthia: Bravo, Edward! Instead of being taken to the cleaners, your making money with your divorce—

Edward: Arlene may have been out of it at first, but now! She is the chair of the LGBTQ support league at the 'Daughters of the American Revolution.' There's talk of it going national with outreach programs in all the major cities. She is getting a lot of mileage from Charlene's Lifestyle choice. The old girl travels with an entourage.

Cynthia: What a cast of characters. If I hadn't heard the same elsewhere, I would think you were making it all up. And what about you? How are you doing? How's the bachelor's life treating you?

Edward: I'm doing great. Never had it so good. Swamped with work, but with interesting cases, so I don't mind. I'm too busy to keep up with Charlene's dramas, and that's a good thing. I try to stay out of all of it. She thinks we're going to get back together one day. She says when things calm down, everything will just go back to normal. Showing concern or offering her help would only be construed to prove her point. I don't want to encourage her.

Cynthia: Maybe the only way to rid yourself of Charlene is to get married again. I'm sure one of New York's most eligible bachelors must be swamped with offers. Playing the field? Seeing someone special? What's your status, gorgeous?

Edward: (enjoying the flirtation, laughing, circling the table) I've been so busy I haven't been able to take advantage of my new circumstances.

Cynthia: All work and no play make for a dull boy. We'll take care of that when I get back to New York. I have always had my eye on you, cowboy.

Edward: (laughing) Have you acquired Venetian tastes as well?

Cynthia: Ogg! . . . We lived there for over a year, and believe me, you acquire it through osmosis. It's in the water, in the air.

Edward: Ah! Something to look forward to! (staring out of the window) But Cynthia, I'm from West Virginia. We're coal miners there--

Cynthia: As rough as cowboys are, they wear tight pants and are a hell of a lot cleaner than coal miners.

Edward: Your right. Let's make it cowboys then. They do have better costumes.

Cynthia: There's a smorgasbord of roles to play, lover, and I'll bet you're good at all of them.

Edward: (laughing) Rumors, rumors. Most of them started by Charlene. What did Charlene tell you? How well I'm hung? Or was it my incredible stamina she praised? She's such a braggart.

Cynthia: First, I'm hearing of it, but it sounds like it MUST be investigated further. You know, I've always wanted to dance naked in that apartment of yours. Removing my veils in the clouds, one by one, bringing ambrosia to Olympus.

(the curtain creeps down slowly as the conversation continues)

Edward: Humm . . . You have gone Venetian.

Cynthia: Like in an Ayn Rand novel. (sighing)

Edward: That's quite a smorgasbord you have.

Cynthia Yes, yes, it is. I'm thinking I'll make you a beta tester for my new lingerie line. Would you like that, Edward?

Edward: When do you leave for New York?

Cynthia: (laughing) Well, in two weeks. I have to make a stop in London, though—

Curtain Falls

Thank you for Reading Opus 2020
Please post a review on Amazon

www.ingramcontent.com/pod-product-compliance
Lightning Source LLC
Chambersburg PA
CBHW052147170626
46812CB00004B/1621